Jaipur rushes out of the trailer  wildflowers tucked in the lush, gree the end of her leash, checking out surroundings. Unfortunately—or maybe fortunately—she completely ignores me.

After about fifteen minutes of enthusiastic exploring, Jaipur lies down in the grass. Tim fills a large metal bowl with water and places it in front of her. I sit on the step of Tim's truck watching Jaipur's pink tongue dip over and over into her water dish.

Sitting there with the trucks, trailers, and tigers, I feel like I've joined the circus.

"Ready to learn how to greet a tiger?" Tim asks me.

Although I hear myself say that I am, I'm not really sure.

"Okay, you're going to approach Jaipur from her side," Tim says. "Once you get close, position your greeting stick by her shoulder. If she tries to get her mouth near you, you'll push her away. If she's behaving, use your other hand to give her firm strokes down her back. Got it?"

"Yes," I say, forcing my voice to sound strong.

"When you're standing next to the tiger," Paul adds, "you'll want to keep the *side* of your body toward the animal, rather than the *front* of your body. That way you don't get eviscerated if the tiger decides to take a swipe at you."

Good to know. I start to have second, or maybe they

are third, thoughts.

"All right then. Go ahead," Tim says.

Jaipur is still lounging, not paying any attention to us. I slowly walk toward her from the side. My heart pounds. My breaths come fast.

Jaipur turns to face me.

"Stop, Jess," Tim says in a low voice. "Don't approach her head-on."

I freeze in place.

Tim continues, "The reason she turned toward you is that you seemed hesitant. If you're anxious, the tiger thinks there's something wrong. It makes her wary. Try again from the side, but be confident."

Just like that, Tim wants me to let go of all of my fears. He wants me to completely disregard the part of my brain that says, *Do not go near a wild animal.* It's the same part of my brain that has kept me alive for sixteen years.

But I do trust Tim. I don't think he wants me to get eviscerated.

I step to Jaipur's side and walk forward, faking a confidence that I don't have. I move closer and closer, forcing anxious thoughts out of my brain. Slowing my nervous breathing. Calming my pounding heart.

WILD ANIMAL SCHOOL

J.W. LYNNE

ISBN 978-1480061996

For my mom and dad, who always encouraged me to pursue my dreams, no matter how silly they seemed.

And for Peter, without whom this book might never have been written.

WILD ANIMAL SCHOOL

Saturday, July 12th

It's six fifty-three in the morning on my sixteenth birthday. I stand outside the battered wooden gate to a compound just off a desolate dirt road. On either side of the gate are high concrete walls. It's impossible to see what's on the other side. *I hope this is the right place.*

And then I hear a low, slow roar. Then another one. And then another one. I smile. *The lions are waking up.*

I take a deep breath and glance down at my brand-new work boots, my thick white socks, my pale shins, and my khaki work shorts and shirt. *I'm ready ... I think.*

I knock on the gate.

There's no answer.

I knock again, a little harder.

Still no answer.

I pull on the gate and, strangely, it opens. I'm surprised they'd leave the gate to a place like this unlocked.

I poke my head inside. "Hello?" I call out.

Suddenly, a barking dog barrels toward me, sharp

white teeth bared. I shove the gate back, planting my foot at the bottom to prevent it from opening any further. The dog's menacing jaw pushes through the gap.

"It's okay," I tell the dog. "I belong here."

The dog stops barking in mid-bark.

A grizzly older man's face appears above the dog's. "Are you sure?" he asks me.

"Hi, I'm—" I start.

"I know who you are. Are those your forms?" He pulls the papers that I clutch in my sweaty hand through the partially-open gate and looks them over. "You're sixteen?"

"Today," I say.

He sighs. "Come in."

I pull the gate toward me enough so that I can enter and shut it behind me. The back of the gate is reinforced with metal bars. I wonder whether that's to keep things in or out. My skin prickles with unease.

The man walks toward a small, rundown shack that has chips of white paint peeling from its worn wooden siding. The dog follows silently by his side, now appearing as harmless as a puppy. I catch up with them inside the shack. The dog crawls under the desk and lies down.

With a dismissive wave of his hand, the man directs me to a rusted chair. "Sit. There are some rules of the ranch that we need to go over." He doesn't look at me when he speaks.

I sit and assess my surroundings. The inner walls of

the shack are almost completely obscured by awards, certificates, and photos of exotic animals—tigers, elephants, leopards, and bears—with people who I assume are their trainers.

I am drawn to the only thing on the wall that doesn't appear to be in danger of being enveloped by the chaos around it: a framed oil painting of a dark-haired woman holding a baby tiger. The cub gazes at the woman with a bright, playful expression. Although tigers can't smile, it almost seems like this one is. The woman's kind, captivating, dark eyes stare out of the painting, appearing to look directly at me.

I force myself to focus my attention on the man as he continues, "The first rule is that you arrive dressed for work. That means work boots and long pants. There are a lot of things here that can scrape you up. You need a layer of protection."

I look down at my bare knees.

"I assume you didn't bring any long pants with you." He pauses, apparently waiting for my response even though his eyes are still focused on his desk.

I shake my head. "No, I didn't—"

"Today, you'll wear these." He tosses some threadbare work pants onto the desk. "Throw them on over your shorts."

I reach for the pants.

He holds up his hand, stopping me. "Not right now,"

he says. "Right now you listen."

I swallow and sit back in my chair. I don't like this man. He must love animals, otherwise why would he work with them for a living? I'd thought I would like anyone who loves animals like I do. I was wrong.

I've been dreaming of being an animal trainer ever since my parents took me to the circus when I was nine years old. I remember watching a man in a sequined vest step into a cage with three tigers. The tigers stood on their hind legs and the man danced with them, one at a time and then all together. It felt like nothing could possibly go wrong there, but here, I feel like it can.

The man goes on, "Next rule is, you never stick your fingers inside the enclosures. These are wild animals here, not pets. Final rule is, you pay attention to the trainers and do exactly as they say, no matter what." The man looks directly into my eyes for the first time. "You got all that?"

"Yes."

"Good," he says, and then he pushes a button and speaks into a radio, "Ryan, I've got the new student. Pick her up in the office."

"Be right there," a younger voice answers.

"Your trainer will be here in a few minutes," the man tells me, and then he goes about his business. He reviews papers and files them. He makes notes. He doesn't say anything to me. I want to excuse myself and wait outside, but the man seems so absorbed by his work that I feel like anything I do will interrupt him. And so I just sit there, completely uncomfortable.

The work pants on the desk smell like animal poop. I don't want to wear them. I wish I'd known about the long pants rule. I hope the trainer is nicer than this man, who never introduced himself. I know from looking at the Bob's Exotic Animal Sanctuary website that he's the ranch's owner, Bob North. He looks different in the picture online than he does in person. The man sitting in front of me looks tired and old.

A guy with a mop of curly reddish-brown hair pops his head into the shack and motions to me. "Come on."

I stand and grab the work pants. "Thank you, Mr. North."

He doesn't look up from his desk. "My name's Bob."

Outside the shack, I quickly pull on the smelly pants and follow the curly-haired guy, who is walking at a pretty good clip up the hill.

I catch up with him. "I'm Jessica," I say.

"Ryan," he responds. "There are four trainers here: me, Tim, Paul, and Leslie. There's also Aaron, who apprentices here. He's Bob's son. I'm gonna give you a tour of the ranch. Does that sound cool?"

"Sounds great!" I feel a wave of relief; already Ryan is much friendlier than Mr. North.

Ryan retrieves a ring of keys from his pocket and unlocks a tall chain-link gate. "We are now entering a secured area. As a student, you always need to be accompanied by a trainer whenever you're in a secured area." Ryan pulls a square of red cloth from a bucket and clips the cloth to the gate. "We put up a red flag to let everyone know that someone's inside. If you see a red flag on a gate, before you open it, you need to communicate with whoever's inside the area to make sure it's safe to enter."

We move through the gate. Ryan locks it behind us and tugs on the lock to make sure it's secure.

I follow him along a remarkably-clean wooden walkway that winds past some animal cages. I peer into the first cage.

Suddenly, a huge tiger leaps from a raised perch inside the cage and lands on the ground just a few feet away from me. Even though the chain-link separates us, I jump back at least a foot, and nearly fall off the walkway.

Ryan grabs my shoulder to steady me. "You can't respond to them like that. Around the animals, you need to stay in control. Stand your ground."

My cheeks flush with embarrassment.

Ryan leads me to other cages, introducing me to tigers, lions, and leopards, one by one. At each cage, he tugs on the lock and points out the water bowl. "Every time you pass an animal, check their water. If it's not full, fill it, and check it again later. Grab the hose. Let's top Lotus off."

I turn on the water and bring the hose to Ryan. He fills

Lotus's bowl, and when he's done, he sprays the water at her. She chases the spray with her open mouth, drinking it, just like our family's dog does. Water droplets on her orange, black, and white fur glisten in the morning sunshine.

Ryan gestures to neighboring tigers that are pacing excitedly. "They want to play too."

He hands me the hose, and I walk from cage to cage, giving each of the tigers a turn with the spray as they prance around. I smile. *The tigers are dancing with me.*

"Okay, enough of that," Ryan says, shutting off the water. "Time to get some work done. Let's go scoop up some elephant poop."

* * *

Two long trunks reach toward me, moving over my body like some sort of strange security scanner. The elephants use the tips of their trunks, like fingers, to check the pockets of my shirt.

"This is Emily and Pongo," Ryan introduces the elephants to me. "They're frisking you."

"Why are you wearing my pants?" a male voice says from behind me.

I'd forgotten that I'm wearing somebody else's pants. Although I haven't looked in the mirror, I'm sure I look like a complete dork with my shirt stuffed into them so they don't fall down.

I turn to see a muscled guy in dusty jeans and a worn gray t-shirt, standing behind me with a wheelbarrow. His brown hair falls in his face.

"Mr. North told me to wear them," I say.

"Whatever," he grumbles as he passes me.

"Let's get some hay," Ryan says, leading me into the barn. "We distract the elephants with food while we scoop up their poop."

"Was that Aaron?" I ask Ryan.

"Yup," he says.

Aaron reminds me of his father.

Ryan and I collect armfuls of hay and emerge into the sunlight to see Emily and Pongo examining the wheelbarrow that Aaron is shoveling full of elephant poop.

"Emily, Pongo, come," Ryan calls out.

Emily glances in our direction and then takes off toward us. She moves surprisingly fast for such a big animal. Pongo follows.

"Trunks up," Ryan instructs as they get close.

The elephants instantly stop walking and curl their trunks up to their foreheads. Ryan and I dump the hay in front of them.

"All right," Ryan tells them.

The elephant's trunks swing down and skillfully pick up bunches of hay. They stuff the food into their mouths and quickly go back for more.

"Grab a wheelbarrow," Ryan says to me.

He picks up two shovels and enters the elephant pen. Although the animals are distracted, there are no bars between him and them. I don't consider whether following Ryan is a good idea or not; I'm too busy awkwardly maneuvering the wobbly wheelbarrow. I've never actually used one of these things before. It's surprisingly difficult to keep it balanced as it moves over the uneven ground. Aaron looks over, barely hiding a smirk, as he effortlessly speeds past me with a full load.

I park my wheelbarrow next to Ryan and he hands me a shovel. Following his lead, I scoop the heavy poop from the ground and plop it into the wheelbarrow.

"Elephant's digestive systems are very inefficient," Ryan explains as we work. "They eat a lot and poop a lot. Even though we only have two elephants, we scoop up a truckload of poop from the elephant pen three times a day."

Thanks to Ryan's efficient work, our wheelbarrow fills quickly. I muscle it up the ramp to the ranch truck, a rusted old thing that looks like it has lived a hard life. When I attempt to dump the poop into the truck bed, I nearly lose my balance. Fortunately, all of the poop lands in the correct place and I don't go with it. Also fortunately, Aaron isn't there to smirk at me.

As I steer the empty wheelbarrow back to the elephant pen, Aaron is already on his way to the ranch truck with another full load. He seems to intentionally cross my path, forcing me to stop.

"So what's your story?" Aaron asks me.

I'm not ready to tell him my story. "What do you mean?"

"You want to be a zookeeper or something?"

I *could* tell him that, when I was nine years old, I decided I was going to be a tiger trainer when I grew up. And that, when I announced this to my parents, my dad laughed at me and insisted that I was going to be a doctor. But that I never lost my desire to work with animals. And that I want to find out what it's like before I go off to college and settle into my life as a future neurosurgeon. And that I wanted this experience so badly that I just spent all but sixty-seven dollars and forty cents of my life savings to try it. Instead, I say, "I don't know yet. I'm only sixteen."

"I'm sixteen, and I know what I want to be," Aaron says.

"It's different when you're going into the family business," I snap, immediately regretting the way I said it.

"Who says I'm going into the family business?" Aaron scoops a nearby pile of poop into his wheelbarrow and wheels away.

* * *

By the time late afternoon arrives, I've filled numerous water dishes; scooped up loads of animal poop; scrubbed cages and walkways; practically inhaled the peanut butter sandwich, apple, and carrots I packed for lunch; and drunk every last drop of my water.

Ryan announces that we need to feed the tigers, lions, and leopards. In the kitchen, he fills my arms with logs of defrosting "Carnivore Diet" sealed in thick plastic and explains, "Carnivore Diet is chopped beef with added vitamins and minerals to provide a nutritionally complete diet for the cats."

I spill the logs onto the counter and, side-by-side with Ryan, slice open each package with a knife and drop the meat into plastic tubs. We pack the tubs in a clean "food-only" wheelbarrow, trudge up to the big cat area, and raise the red flag.

The animals seem to know why we're here. As soon as they see us enter, they begin feverishly pacing and vocalizing intensely, transformed from the playful cats I met this morning into intimidating beasts.

"Follow me with the wheelbarrow," Ryan instructs. "We've gotta be quick."

Rapidly, he moves from cage to cage, tossing meat into each feeding trough with a splat, as I try my best to keep up with him. Each cat gets an appropriate amount of food for his or her weight. Most of the tigers get one log. Some of the bigger males get one and a half logs. Ryan knows the amounts by heart.

The cats growl deeply at us as they receive their meal, a natural instinct to protect their catch.

"Never attempt to take anything back," Ryan warns

me. "If you make a mistake, you live with it."

When we're finished, the growls subside as the animals wolf down their food. We head back to the exit with our empty wheelbarrow. As we pass the cages, we are careful not to get too close and make animals that haven't finished eating feel threatened.

One of the lions stares at her untouched food. Even I know that isn't normal.

Ryan approaches her, and she doesn't growl. "What's wrong Savannah? Not hungry?"

The lion just looks at him.

Ryan presses his lips together as if he's trying not to say something. He grabs his radio and reluctantly speaks, "Bob, Savannah's not eating. Do you want me to take a look at her?"

"I'll be right up," a gruff voice responds.

Seconds later, Mr. North comes charging into the big cat area. Without acknowledging us, he walks straight to Savannah's cage, opens her lock, steps inside, and shuts the door behind him. Savannah affectionately rubs against him, just like a housecat.

She likes him.

"Let's fill the water bowls and check the locks," Ryan whispers to me.

I go with Ryan to continue our chores, but I keep an eye on Savannah.

"Lie down," Mr. North says to her.

Savannah does.

Mr. North presses on her belly, disguising it as a tummy rub. Savannah is obviously enjoying it; she rolls onto her back with her huge paws batting at the air. I can't help smiling.

"That's a good girl," Mr. North tells the lion, then he raises his voice, obviously talking to Ryan even though he looks only at Savannah, "She'll stay separate from her pride tonight. Plenty of water. I'll check her again later."

"Got it," Ryan answers.

Mr. North leaves just as quickly as he came.

"Our lions spend the night in pride groups—one male with each group of females," Ryan explains to me. "That's how they'd be in the wild."

There are two large cages—one for each pride group. Ryan and I slide open the gates that connect the individual cages to the large ones. The lions race to join their pride groups and greet one another by touching their heads together or rubbing against one another's sides.

As Mr. North instructed, Savannah is left alone in her individual cage with a bowl full of water that she eagerly drinks.

The radio crackles, and a voice I don't recognize says, "Hey, Ryan, does the student want to walk the elephants?"

My eyes widen. I smile and nod.

"Why, yes, she does," Ryan tells the radio.

A tall guy, with wavy blond hair pulled back into a ponytail and a smile that makes me feel less self-conscious than I normally do, extends his hand to me. "I'm Tim."

"I'm Jessica," I say, allowing his strong, calloused hand to embrace mine.

"Have you ever walked an elephant before?" he asks me.

I shake my head. "Never."

"Let's remedy that, shall we?" Tim smiles again, his blue eyes appearing to illuminate when he does.

I smile back. "Okay."

"We're going to take them out to the field." Tim gestures to a dirt path lined with trees that leads away from the ranch. "There are lots of small saplings along the way that the elephants like to uproot, so we need to have them hold someone's arm with their trunk as we exit the ranch. You ask them to hold your arm by saying 'Arm' and putting your arm like this." Tim extends his arm, bent at the elbow, like an old-fashioned gentleman does for a lady. "You try it."

"Arm," I say, positioning my arm like Tim did.

Tim wraps his arm around my arm, exactly like I imagine an elephant's trunk might do. I laugh.

"Good," he says. "Now let's do it for real." He opens the latch on the elephants' gate. A twinge of fear mixed with excitement tickles through me.

"Need help?" a young male voice calls out. I turn and see Aaron and the ranch dog, Joyce, coming toward us.

"You want to take Pongo?" Tim calls back.

"Sure," Aaron says. "Pongo, come."

Pongo lumbers toward him.

Just when the massive animal gets close, Aaron instructs, "Arm."

Pongo takes Aaron's arm, and they amble together down the path. Joyce trots along behind them, tail wagging happily.

"Do it just like that," Tim says to me.

"Emily, come," I say.

Emily doesn't move.

"Try *inviting* her," Tim suggests.

I soften my tone and try again. "Emily, come."

Emily charges straight toward me. My excitement transforms to pure fear.

"Stand to her right," Tim guides.

Tim doesn't sound nervous. I try to let that fact calm me as I move to the right of what I predict will be Emily's path. Emily picks up speed. If she decides to barrel past me, I won't be able to stop her.

"Arm," I say. Hoping for the best, I offer my arm.

Emily reaches toward me with her trunk and wraps it around my elbow. I start moving involuntarily as Emily carries me onward. Tim grabs a bag of apples from a bench near the elephant barn, and catches up with us.

Emily leads the way, past the trees and into a grassy open area, about the size of a football field. Pongo is already there, wandering at the far end with Aaron. Joyce chases butterflies nearby.

"Tell Emily 'Go play,'" Tim whispers in my ear.

When I say those words, Emily immediately lets go of my arm and prances off. I've never seen an elephant walk like that; she appears … happy. Emily finds a clump of tall grass, easily uproots it, and stuffs it into her mouth. Tim reaches into his bag and pulls out an apple. He tosses it into the grass near Emily. She retrieves it and places it into her mouth.

"How's your throwing arm?" Tim asks me.

"Not too good," I admit.

He hands me an apple. "Then you throw to Emily."

I toss the apple close enough to Emily that she goes after it. Tim hurls one across the field, incredibly close to Pongo. Pongo grabs it and tosses it into his mouth.

Aaron sits on a rock and lights a cigarette.

"Aaron smokes?" I ask Tim, although I suppose the answer is obvious.

"Only out here. There's no smoking allowed on the ranch," Tim says. "You smoke?"

"No," I say, my face wrinkling with disgust. "Smoking is gross."

"Yeah, it is," Tim's hand brushes his shirt pocket where a package of cigarettes peeks out.

For some reason I feel comfortable asking him, "Then why do you do it?"

"I started when I was twelve. My dad smoked. He always told me not to, but I saw him doing it, and I wanted to be just like him. Now I know better. Dads aren't perfect, you know."

"Mine wasn't. He's part of the reason why I'm here," I say. And then, for some reason—maybe because I feel like I can trust Tim, even though I hardly know him—I tell him about the tiger trainer who I saw at the circus when I was a kid, and how my dad laughed at me when I said that I wanted to be a tiger trainer too. And how, a few days later, my dad left for work and never came home. He was in a horrible car accident. He died instantly. The ambulance didn't even take him to the hospital, because the paramedics knew he couldn't be saved. From that day on, my mom has spent most of her time alone in her bedroom. And so, in a way, I lost both my parents that day.

Strangely, sharing these details of my life with Tim doesn't feel nearly as uncomfortable as it should. When I finally stop talking, he says, "I'm sorry about your dad. You did the right thing by doing this. You won't regret it."

My eyes well up with tears. I'm sure Tim notices, but he doesn't mention it. If he did, I'm certain the tears would start to flow. I take a deep breath—trying to will away my tears—and stare across the field at Emily and Pongo. Pongo bounds off. Emily follows. Watching the elephants wander around, as free as wild animals should be, with no gates or bars to hold them in, I wonder aloud if they'll ever come back to us.

"They always do," Tim tells me.

Almost on cue, Emily heads toward us looking majestic, her huge ears spread like wings. She walks right up to me and begins examining my face with her curious trunk. I stroke her mud-caked skin; she feels like a soft tree trunk. Emily is standing so close to me that I can feel humid heat coming from her mouth each time she exhales. I look up at her sharp, intimidating tusks. *I've never been this close to an elephant before.*

"Is this safe?" I ask Tim.

"Pretty much," Tim says.

Despite his lack of complete reassurance, I don't step away.

A lone car driving along the dirt road next to the field pulls to a stop. The driver leans out of the car window, eyes practically bulging from his head. "Are those *your* elephants?" he calls out to us.

Tim nods. "Yup."

The man shakes his head in disbelief. "You mind if I …" He pulls out his cell phone.

"Go ahead," Tim says.

I look up at the elephant towering over me and whisper, so softly that it's almost to myself, "Does this *ever* get old?" I can't imagine how it could, even if I did this every day for the rest of my life.

Tim answers just as softly, "Absolutely not."

Saturday, July 19th

Today, I arrive at the ranch prepared. I wear long pants and a long-sleeved shirt. In a small cooler, I have a big lunch, plus snacks and extra water. In a brown paper bag, I have Aaron's work pants—the smelly pants that I pulled on one week ago at Mr. North's insistence; I had to wash them three times to get rid of the awful stink.

Joyce meets me at the gate. She barks at me, but her barks are friendly.

"Hey, Joyce, where is everyone?" I brush the dirt from her thick black fur, although I probably shouldn't bother; she can't possibly stay clean here.

Joyce leads me to the elephant enclosure, where Tim and Ryan are filling wheelbarrows with poop.

"Oh shoot!" Tim says as soon as he sees me. "Didn't someone call you?"

"Oh shoot!" wasn't the kind of greeting I was hoping for. "No. Why?" I ask.

"We were going to reschedule you. We have a job

today." Tim explains that they're going to take some of the animals to be part of a movie filming. Mr. North accepted the job because it paid a lot of money; it's expensive to feed and care for all of these animals. Tim gives me a choice: I can stay and go to the movie shoot with them, or I can leave and reschedule the day. I've never been to a movie set, and it sounds exciting, so I decide to stay.

"If you're staying, grab a shovel," Tim says.

I get a shovel and join Tim, who is working at triple his normal speed. I shovel up poop as fast as I can, but my speed doesn't even come close to matching his. I don't talk. I don't want anything to slow me down.

"Go ahead and dump this," Tim says to me. He turns away from the nearly-full wheelbarrow and starts piling shovelfuls of poop into Ryan's.

I like how Tim and Ryan treat me as part of the team even though most of the time I'm probably more of a hindrance than a help.

Carefully, I maneuver Tim's wheelbarrow away. I don't want to accidentally dump my load on the way to the truck. I'm concentrating so hard that I almost run into Aaron.

"Hey!" He sounds annoyed.

"Hi." I try to be pleasant. "I brought back your pants." I tilt my head toward the bench by the elephant barn where I left them. "I washed them."

He doesn't stop walking. "Thanks."

I hope Aaron isn't coming to the movie set.

I dump the elephant poop into the ranch truck bed, kicking the side of the wheelbarrow to get rid of every last bit of my load. As I wheel back, I remember that I forgot to ask about Savannah. The last time I saw her, the lion had refused her dinner. "Not eating can be a serious sign that something is wrong with an animal," Ryan had told me.

I take a deep breath—preparing myself for whatever the answer might be—and ask Ryan, "How's Savannah?"

"Why do you ask?" Tim responds, looking at Ryan with narrowed eyes.

"She refused her dinner last Saturday," I explain, feeling worried.

"She's fine," Ryan answers quickly, returning Tim's stare.

"Good." I breathe a hesitant sigh of relief. *If Savannah is fine, why did Tim and Ryan act so strange when I asked about her?*

Tim's radio crackles and a tense male voice asks, "Can I get some help crating the cats?"

"Be right up," Tim says into his radio, and then he calls out to Ryan, who is speeding away with a full wheelbarrow, "Jess and I are going to help Paul."

"Cool," Ryan shouts back.

I park the empty wheelbarrow outside the elephant enclosure—well out of reach of curious trunks—and run after Tim.

"Pongo and Jaipur are working on the movie today," Tim tells me as I catch up with him. *If I remember correctly, Jaipur is one of the older tigers.* Tim continues, "We're going to bring Lotus too. It'll be her first trip away from the ranch. It's important to expose the animals to as many different experiences as possible, especially when they're young, that way new things don't spook them so much."

A stocky, balding man in well-worn work pants and a dusty, brown Bob's Exotic Animal Sanctuary t-shirt meets Tim and me in the big cat area.

"Jessica, this is Paul," Tim introduces us.

"Hey," Paul says reflexively. He hands Tim and I each a wooden stick.

I'm not sure why I need a stick.

"Eventually, we'll teach you how to leash a tiger," Tim says to me, "but we're in a rush this morning, so just watch for now." He glances at the stick that I hold uncertainly. "Use the greeting stick as an extension of your body. If an animal gets too close for comfort, you can use it, instead of your hand, to push them away."

Tim and Paul open Jaipur's door and enter her home. The tiger strides over to Tim and rubs against him—like Savannah did to Mr. North. Paul uses the distraction to slip a chain leash around the Jaipur's neck and fasten it. Paul made it appear less challenging than leashing my family's dog.

"Follow us down to the truck," Tim instructs me. "*Do not* get in front of us. If Jaipur tries to get close to you, put your greeting stick by her shoulder."

Tim opens the door to Jaipur's enclosure and the tiger stalks out quickly with a graceful, wild gait.

"Easy," Paul says to slow her down.

Tim unlocks the outer gate to the big cat area, and Jaipur heads down the hill, fast.

"Easy," Paul reminds her.

Jaipur slows down a little.

Paul guides Jaipur toward an open trailer hooked up to a clean, sparkling pickup truck and says, "In your crate."

Jaipur glances back toward Paul.

"In your crate," Paul repeats in a softer voice.

Jaipur leaps into the trailer. Paul releases her leash, locks the trailer, and heads back up the hill. Tim and I follow.

Paul and Tim go to Lotus's enclosure and enter with a leash. Lotus circles them a few times. She seems to be a bit more of a challenge to leash than Jaipur. In one quick move, Tim reaches out, slips the chain around the tiger's neck, and secures it. I walk behind Tim and Paul as they take Lotus down the hill. When she arrives at the trailer attached to a second nice, new pickup truck, Lotus stops and sniffs at the trailer door, mouth open. Although she looks fully-grown, Tim indicated that Lotus is a young tiger. I wonder if she's ever been inside a trailer before, but

I don't ask any questions. This seems like a critical time.

"In your crate," Paul says to her.

Lotus stays outside the door, sniffing, looking hesitant.

Tim grabs a baby bottle from the passenger seat of the truck and pushes the nipple through one of the trailer's small barred windows. "Lotus, in your crate," Tim says.

Lotus slowly enters the trailer and makes her way to the bottle.

"Good girl," Tim tells her as she sucks down the milk, and Paul secures the trailer door.

"I'm going to head out," Paul tells Tim. "Do you need me to take the student?"

"Nah," Tim says, tossing the nearly-empty milk bottle inside a cooler. "Jess'll ride with me."

"Cool." Paul jumps into the driver's seat of the first truck and starts the engine.

"How far away is the movie set?" I ask Tim as Paul drives off with Jaipur in tow.

"About an hour," he says.

I climb into the passenger side of Tim's truck, feeling relieved that I get to ride with Tim rather than Paul. But it's more than just relief that I feel. The idea of spending an hour chatting with Tim makes me giddy.

* * *

The drive to the set gives us expansive views of towering green mountains and reflective lakes rippled by tiny boats.

25

The hour-long ride seems to go by in mere minutes thanks to a conversation that never dies. We talk about the clouds, the mountains, the animals, and whatever pops into our minds. Strangely, we skip most of the usual getting-to-know-you questions, I think that's because, although we hardly know each other, I feel like I've known him forever.

I know we've arrived at the movie set when I see Pongo's huge trailer parked in a large grassy area. Pongo is busily uprooting and tasting the weeds. A woman sits on his back, her long, golden hair blowing in the wind.

"Is that one of the actresses?" I ask Tim.

He laughs. "No. That's Leslie, one of our trainers."

A police officer steps up to Tim's truck. Tim rolls down the driver's side window.

"We're here for *Mirror Lake*," Tim tells the officer.

"What have you got in the trailer?" the officer asks.

"A tiger," Tim says matter-of-factly.

The officer peeks inside one of the trailer windows. When he catches a glimpse of Lotus, he jumps back. "Check in with the one of the PA's at basecamp. They'll tell you where your holding area will be."

"Will do!" Tim replies.

We bump over the rocky dirt road that cuts through the field. In a clearing filled with RV's and tents, a man wearing a headset that reminds me of the ones telephone operators wear approaches us.

"Tiger?" the man asks.

"Yup," Tim says.

"We have you in that roped-off area down the hill where your partner's set up. Is that good?"

Tim nods. "Perfect."

We follow the flattened-grass tire tracks to our holding area, where we find Paul lounging in the driver's seat of his truck—his feet on the dash—drinking a soda. He tosses the bottle into a cooler and jumps out to meet us.

Without any greetings or small talk, Paul suggests, "Let's acclimate Jaipur, then we can do the same for Lotus."

"Sounds good," Tim says. He parks the truck, and we jump out.

Tim tells me where to stand—so I won't be in the way—and hands me a greeting stick—just in case I need it. He and Paul put Jaipur on a long leash, and Tim invites her to "go play."

Jaipur rushes out of the trailer and breathes in the wildflowers tucked in the lush, green grass. She walks to the end of her leash, checking out every bit of her new surroundings. Unfortunately—or maybe fortunately—she completely ignores me.

After about fifteen minutes of enthusiastic exploring, Jaipur lies down in the grass. Tim fills a large metal bowl with water and places it in front of her. I sit on the step of Tim's truck watching Jaipur's pink tongue dip over and over into her water dish.

Sitting there with the trucks, trailers, and tigers, I feel like I've joined the circus.

"Ready to learn how to greet a tiger?" Tim asks me.

Although I hear myself say that I am, I'm not really sure.

"Okay, you're going to approach Jaipur from her side," Tim says. "Once you get close, position your greeting stick by her shoulder. If she tries to get her mouth near you, you'll push her away. If she's behaving, use your other hand to give her firm strokes down her back. Got it?"

"Yes," I say, forcing my voice to sound strong.

"When you're standing next to the tiger," Paul adds, "you'll want to keep the *side* of your body toward the animal, rather than the *front* of your body. That way you don't get eviscerated if the tiger decides to take a swipe at you."

Good to know. I start to have second, or maybe they are third, thoughts.

"All right then. Go ahead," Tim says.

Jaipur is still lounging, not paying any attention to us. I slowly walk toward her from the side. My heart pounds. My breaths come fast.

Jaipur turns to face me.

"Stop, Jess," Tim says in a low voice. "Don't approach her head-on."

I freeze in place.

Tim continues, "The reason she turned toward you is

that you seemed hesitant. If you're anxious, the tiger thinks there's something wrong. It makes her wary. Try again from the side, but be confident."

Just like that, Tim wants me to let go of all of my fears. He wants me to completely disregard the part of my brain that says, *Do not go near a wild animal.* It's the same part of my brain that has kept me alive for sixteen years.

But I do trust Tim. I don't think he wants me to get eviscerated.

I step to Jaipur's side and walk forward, faking a confidence that I don't have. I move closer and closer, forcing anxious thoughts out of my brain. Slowing my nervous breathing. Calming my pounding heart. Soon I'm near enough to place my greeting stick at Jaipur's shoulder. Then I'm near enough to touch her.

I watch my hand glide over Jaipur's orange and black stripes. Her fur is softer than I'd imagined it would be, like the fur of a puppy, rather than a full-grown dog. I stroke her more deeply, feeling the strong muscles of her back against my fingers. Dogs don't have muscles like that.

Jaipur's beautiful tiger eyes look up into mine, and a warm shiver runs down my spine.

"Good girl," I whisper to her.

Suddenly, Jaipur leaps up. Her attention isn't focused on me. She sees something in the grass. It might be a mouse, or an insect, or the wind. She bolts over to investigate.

"Good job!" Tim says to me. "You didn't even flinch." His voice brings me back to reality: *I just pet a tiger!*

* * *

Jaipur's search for small prey turns up empty. Once she settles back down, Tim calls her into her trailer, and Paul secures the door. Then Tim and Paul leash Lotus and let her out onto the grass. Lotus moves slowly, taking in the scents. She walks to the end of her leash and watches tiny cars on the highway in the distance. Maybe she thinks they're little bugs that she can pounce on.

Tim taps a large, flat rock with his greeting stick and calls, "Lotus, on your seat."

Lotus comes to him and hops onto the rock. Tim rewards her with a small chunk of meat.

Tim touches a stick in the grass. "On your mark."

Lotus jumps off of the rock and walks to the stick. She stops when her two front paws are practically touching it.

"Lie down," Tim says.

Lotus immediately drops onto her belly, right in place.

"All right!" Tim says.

Lotus strides off to watch the little cars again.

"Cueing their behaviors can be calming for the animals when they're faced with an unfamiliar situation," Tim explains to me. He pours some water into a bowl for Lotus. Then he asks me, "Are you hungry?"

Even though I brought my lunch with me, Tim

suggests that I go to "craft service"—the snack area for the people working on the movie. I walk up the hill and, after asking a woman with a headset for directions, find the place called craft service.

Set out on three big tables, there are packages of cookies and chips, fresh fruits and veggies, fancy little cupcakes and brownies, nuts, and practically every other snack anyone could desire. I see why Tim sent me here.

A thin, blond woman strolls over and picks up a small pink cupcake with glitter sprinkles. "These are heavenly!" she says to no one in particular. She pops the treat into her mouth, whole. "Yummy!"

After the woman leaves, I make a meal out of nuts, fruits, and veggies—plus two yummy pink cupcakes for desert.

* * *

When the movie people call for Jaipur, Paul jumps into his truck and drives her trailer up the hill. Tim and I follow in his truck—with Lotus's trailer.

"If Jaipur gets tired or full of food rewards," Tim tells me, "we can switch her out with Lotus." Even though Lotus is younger and slightly smaller than Jaipur, I doubt most people would be able to tell the difference between them unless the two tigers were standing side-by-side.

Tim and Paul park the trucks close to the set, and we hop out.

A heavyset man with a two-way radio holstered on his belt greets us, "I'm Doug, the first AD. Let's have you talk to the director. He's over in video village."

Leslie and Ryan join us, and we walk toward a half-occupied collection of director's chairs that face two large video monitors. Doug leads us to the man who is sitting front row center, focused intensely on the monitors. The man leans back as we approach.

"These are the animal trainers," Doug tells the director. He includes me in that group, even though I'm completely unworthy of the title.

"Thank you so much for coming," the director says as if it is a true privilege to meet us. "The scene we're filming today is a dream sequence. Our father is dreaming that he's in a jungle. He steps into a clearing, and there are wild animals staring at him. Then his daughter appears and says, 'Dad,' and our father says to her, 'What are you doing here?' and she says, 'In our house?' and then the dream fades away. It would be nice if, when the daughter walks into the scene, the animals acknowledge her in some way."

"No problem," Tim says.

"Great," Doug says, and he walks us away from the director. He turns to Tim. "I understand that, for safety reasons, we have to film the tiger and the elephant separately. We'd like to do the elephant's coverage first."

"Sure," Tim says.

"Awesome." Doug peels off.

As the rest of us walk toward the animal trailers, Tim puts his hand on my shoulder and presents me to Leslie. "Leslie, this is Jessica. She's our new student."

"You brought a *student*?" Leslie asks under her breath, but loud enough for me to hear.

"Today is one of the days she was signed up for," Tim says.

Leslie throws on a smile and glances at me. "Nice to meet you." Her smile disappears quickly.

Tim and Paul help Ryan and Leslie get Pongo out of the trailer and in position in front of the cameras. Once Pongo is settled, Tim, Paul, and I go back to video village.

A woman wearing a lacy, white nightgown—the same woman who I saw earlier at the craft service table—approaches the set and exclaims so loudly that I can hear her from video village, "Whoa! That's a real elephant!" She marches over to the director. "So what exactly is going to happen here?" she asks him in an annoyed voice.

I can't hear the director's response, but the woman—who I assume is playing the daughter in the scene—doesn't seem happy with it.

"Okay, let's shoot this!" she yells, rolling her eyes. She gives Pongo a wide berth as she takes a position near one of the cameras.

"Action!" shouts the director.

A male actor—dressed in safari gear—enters the clearing. He looks at Pongo and then at the place where I assume that Jaipur will eventually be. Then the actress walks into the clearing. Pongo reaches toward her and sniffs her with his trunk, like he did to me on my first day at the ranch.

"That's great," the director purrs. "I love that!"

"Oh, no, no, no!" the actress shrieks, backing away from Pongo.

"Cut!" the director sighs.

"We can't have it reaching at me like that. It's freaking me out," the actress shouts to the director.

It's weird to hear her refer to Pongo as "it."

The director hurries over to her. "It looks great when he does that."

"Well, I can't do the scene like this," she says.

"Okay, let's do it again without the trunk action," the director appeases her.

"You got that?" Doug calls out to Ryan and Leslie. "No trunk action this time."

"Got it," Leslie responds.

The actress huffs and returns to her place by the camera.

"Action," the director says softly.

The male actor enters the clearing. Then the actress takes a few steps forward. "Dad?" she mutters.

Pongo begins to reach toward her.

"Trunk down," Leslie instructs him.

Pongo puts his trunk down immediately. But it's too

late; the actress is already charging toward the director. She's breathing fast and deep. The director meets her halfway.

"I can't do this," she says, and then she turns and marches off toward the RVs.

"I'm sorry," Leslie says to the director.

"It's not your fault," he responds with an exhale.

"Do you want to shoot this using the stand-in instead?" Doug suggests to the director. "We can digitally replace her face."

"The stand-in looks nothing like her," the director growls. "Tomorrow, I want a stand-in who bears some resemblance to our actress."

I follow the director's gaze to the 'stand-in' woman. He's right; she doesn't look anything at all like the actress. The actress looks more like … me.

When I look back, the director is looking at me. "Let's use her," he says.

Everyone looks at me.

"She's just a student," Leslie says, looking flustered.

"That's fine," he says, and then he turns to me. "Are you okay with the elephant sniffing you and the tiger doing whatever it is he's going to do?"

"Yeah," I say.

"Get her to hair and wardrobe," the director orders. "We'll shoot the elephant's coverage while we're waiting."

The crewmembers immediately get to work moving

the cameras and lights.

Doug leads me to a woman with short pigtails—who wears one of the ubiquitous movie-people headsets—and tells her, "Take this young lady to hair."

The woman directs me toward the RVs. "I'll get you a contract, and we're going to need a copy of your driver's license."

"Can I have a second?" I ask.

"You can have a *second*," she says uneasily.

I go to Tim and Leslie and say quietly, "They want to see my driver's license, but I just turned sixteen, I haven't got—"

"You're sixteen!" Leslie says in a panicked whisper.

"Seriously?" Tim adds.

"I thought you knew that," I say. "My mom signed the consent form for the ranch—"

"We can't bring minors to movie sets with the animals. If they found out …" Tim runs his hand through his hair.

I really want to be in the movie, even if they are going to digitally replace my face, but I don't want anyone to get in trouble. "What do you want me to do?" I ask Tim.

Leslie hands me her wallet. "You're Leslie. You're nineteen."

I look to Tim for the answer.

Tim hardly makes eye contact. "Okay."

I stuff Leslie's wallet into my pocket. As I walk away,

I look back at Tim. He's staring at the ground.

The pigtailed woman meets up with me. "Sorry, I didn't introduce myself before. I'm Beth. What's your name?"

"I'm Leslie," I hear myself say.

* * *

I spend the next few minutes in a fantasy. A hairdresser uses a blow dryer and curling iron to make my hair look almost exactly like the actress's. Everyone keeps saying how much I look like her. I know they just mean my hair, but having any part of me compared to a beautiful movie star feels good.

When the hairdressers are through, Beth retrieves me and takes me to an RV that she refers to as "your trailer." I step inside and find a couch and a large flat-screen TV. There's even a small bathroom. It reminds me of a tiny hotel room, without the bed.

Hanging in the mini-closet is the beautiful nightgown and the slippers that the actress was wearing. I can't believe I'm actually going to get to wear them. I undress and pull the nightgown over my head, careful not to mess up my perfectly-arranged hair. I slide on the slippers and admire myself in the full-length mirror. *I look like a princess.*

When I open my trailer door, Beth is outside waiting for me. "Perfect!" she says when she sees me. She brings me to Doug and announces, "Here's our photo double."

"Excellent," he says. As Doug walks us toward the cameras, he tells me, "I want you to do the scene exactly how we showed you. We're putting you on a contract, so go ahead and say the lines too."

Beth takes me to the spot by the camera where the actress stood. She points out a small stick on the ground in the clearing. "When I cue you, go to your mark."

The director yells, "Action!"

My heart pounds. Beth taps my shoulder. I walk forward and stand behind the stick. Pongo reaches toward me. I look at him, then I turn to "my dad."

"Cut!" the director orders. He walks over to me and says with a gentle smile, "You aren't part of the dream. You don't see the animals. Just ignore them. You're in the living room of your house."

I feel like I should have known that. "Okay. I'm sorry." *I just ruined my very first take.*

"Going again," someone says.

"Take two," someone else says.

Beth brings me back behind the camera.

"Action!" the director bellows.

I step forward, ignoring Pongo. Unfortunately, he ignores me too.

"Dad?" I say anyway.

"Cut!" The director isn't happy.

The first take would have been perfect if I hadn't looked at Pongo.

I hear Ryan tell the director, "I'm on it!"

Ryan runs over to me. I start to apologize. Ryan stops me.

"You're doing fine," he says. He holds an apple up in the air. Pongo watches as Ryan slips it inside the sleeve of my nightgown. "Once the director says, 'Cut,' give the apple to Pongo."

"We're ready," Beth calls out.

"Action!" the director says.

My heart rises into my throat. My ears burn. Everything blurs out of view except for what is right in front of me.

Beth taps my shoulder. I step forward. Pongo reaches for me.

"Dad?" I say.

"What are you doing here?" the actor says.

"In our house?" I ask.

"Cut! Print! One more!" The director sounds thrilled.

I hand Pongo the apple. He tosses it into his mouth and swings his trunk back for more.

"In a minute, Pongo," I tell him.

"That was perfect," Beth says to me. "The director loved it."

Ryan slides another apple up my sleeve. "Good job!" he tells me.

After the next take, the director leaps out of his chair. "Cut! Print! Check the gate! The tiger's up next."

I give Pongo the apple from my sleeve, and then Leslie and Ryan lead him back to his trailer.

"You can go to your trailer," Beth offers, "or you can wait in video village. It won't be too long."

"I guess I'll wait in video village."

Beth walks me to the director's chairs. She gestures to a chair in the back row that says "Cast" on it. "You can sit there."

I climb into the chair and watch as the director consults in hushed tones with various people. After speaking with one man, the director calls out, "Video playback!" A few moments later, the scene that we just filmed appears on the monitors as seen from two different angles. It's hard to believe that the person in the nightgown is actually me. It's strangely disconcerting to see myself in the movie.

After the scene finishes, the monitors mercifully go back to real time. Tim and Paul bring Jaipur into position.

"We're ready for you," Beth says to me.

I follow her back to my spot next to one of the cameras.

Tim comes over to me. "The director would like to have Jaipur look at you when you enter the scene. The way we'll do that is that I'll be just past you, off-camera. I'm going to tell her, 'Eyes, Jaipur;' that should make her look at me, which will make it look as if she's looking at you. It *is* possible that she'll decide to *come* to me instead. If that happens, I'll call her to a mark near me. You should just step out of the way."

I feel quivers of anxiety rise up into my chest. "What if she comes to *me*?"

"Then you point toward *me* and say, 'On your mark.' I have the treat, so she should be more interested in coming to me than you."

"Okay." I say. I'm much less comfortable with the tigers than the elephants. It was only two hours ago that I passed Tiger Greeting 101. My heart begins to pound again.

"Action!" the director exclaims.

I step forward. "Dad?"

"Eyes, Jaipur," I hear Tim say.

"What are you doing here?" the male actor asks.

"In our house?" I ask.

"Cut. Print. Go again," the director says quietly.

Paul gives Jaipur a hunk of beef. I didn't look at Jaipur during the scene, so I have no idea how she did. I glance over at Tim who smiles and nods. I smile back and go join Beth.

"Action!" the director says.

I take a deep breath, finally enjoying my moment in the spotlight. *I feel like a real actress.*

Beth taps me and I step forward.

"Dad?" I say.

"Eyes, Jaipur," I hear Tim murmur.

"What are you doing here?" the other actor asks me.

There is a hint of concern on his face.

"Jaipur, on your mark," I hear Tim say firmly.

I turn and see Jaipur walking—mouth open—in my direction. My heart pounds furiously against my ribs. I jump out of Jaipur's way, but she keeps coming toward me. My heart beats faster. I point to Tim, but I can't make myself speak.

Tim taps a rock with his stick, making a loud smack. "Jaipur, on your mark."

Jaipur looks at Tim and then at me. A large string of drool drips from her mouth.

Tim taps the rock again. Jaipur snaps her attention back to him. She trots off to Tim. He gives her a treat. I exhale with relief.

I feel like I need to sit down, but there's nowhere to sit, and so I stay standing on my trembling legs, hoping that the nightgown hides the shaking.

"Cut! Print." The director walks over to Tim. "I might be able to use pieces of that take. But is it safe to do another one?"

"Why don't we use Lotus?" Tim suggests.

"Whatever you think," the director agrees.

Ryan and Leslie rush over to help Tim and Paul trade Lotus for Jaipur. They work together so easily that it appears they've done this a thousand times.

Once Lotus is settled in position, the director calls, "Action!"

"Dad?"

"Eyes, Lotus."

"What are you doing here?"

"In our house?"

"Cut. Print. Check the gate." The director sounds ecstatic.

"If the gate's good, you can go change," Beth tells me.

I wonder what *gate* she's referring to. I look at Tim and Paul for a clue. They stay in position.

Beth covers her ear with her hand, listening to her headset. Then she smiles. "Gate's good. You're wrapped!"

Alone, I walk to my trailer. I carefully remove the lacy nightgown and put on my dirty ranch clothes. Then I fill out the pile of paperwork waiting for me, using the information that I find in Leslie's wallet. A guy—who looks like he's my age, but must be at least eighteen—stops by and checks the completed paperwork. Once he's done, he tells me that my colleagues are waiting for me in video village.

When I arrive back on the set, Tim and Paul are directing Lotus through her close-ups. During one take, she cocks her head slightly when she turns to look "at me." It's adorable.

The sun is starting to dip behind a mountain when the director declares, "That's a wrap. Great day, everyone!" He puts his arm over my shoulders. "And a special thanks to our animal trainers and our photo double!"

The crewmembers applaud and then quickly go to

work putting away their equipment.

The director turns to me. "You really saved us today!"

I feel so proud. *A big movie director is thanking me for working on his movie!*

"You know," he continues, "I never got your name."

I catch myself just in time. "Leslie," I say.

"Thanks, Leslie," he says.

My pride turns to shame.

* * *

"We can't tell anyone what happened today" are the first words Tim says to me on our ride back to the ranch. We've been driving on the highway for at least twenty minutes before he says that. "Not Bob. Not Aaron. Not your mom or your friends. Just the five of us know, and it needs to stay that way. Okay?"

"Okay," I say quietly.

And then it is silent again. Tim just drives, following the taillights ahead of us down the dark highway. He doesn't bother to turn on the radio or anything. I watch the shadowy mountains go by and stare at the moon. It stares back.

"I'm sorry, Jess," Tim finally says, his jaw tight. "I'm sorry you had to lie."

I feel bad about lying, but I feel even worse seeing how Tim feels.

Tim goes on, "Even though Leslie's name is on the

paperwork, you're still going to get paid."

"I don't care about the money."

"Leslie will cash the check and give you the cash," Tim continues. "They put you on an actor contract, so once the movie goes to DVD, TV, airplanes, and stuff, she'll probably get residual checks. I'll make sure that money gets to you too."

"Okay," I say.

Tim glances at me. "Did you at least have a good time today?"

A smile grows on my face. "I got to be in a movie, even if they are going to digitally replace my face. And I got to pet a tiger; that was incredible. So, yes, I had a good day."

"I'm glad."

I finally feel like I can ask, "Just out of curiosity, how old did you think I was?"

"Eighteen or nineteen."

I'm flattered.

"That's how old most of our students are," he adds.

I'm less flattered.

It's none of my business, but I ask, "How old are you?"

"Twenty."

"Oh," I say without meaning to.

"'Oh' what?" Tim asks.

"I guess I felt like we were the same age," I say.

"I did too," Tim says.

We spend the rest of our trip absorbed in the same kind of easy conversation that we had on the way over. When we get back to the ranch, I sleepily watch Tim and Paul move Lotus and Jaipur back to their enclosures. Then Tim walks me to the parking lot.

"See you next Saturday," I say as I hop onto my bike.

"Is that how you're getting home?" Tim asks.

"Yeah," I say. "I can't drive yet, remember?"

"Want a ride?"

* * *

I climb into Tim's truck and watch, in the rearview mirror, as he lifts my bike into the back. A moment later, he slides into the driver's seat. "Where are we headed?"

"Camp Charlie."

"What's 'Camp Charlie'?" Tim asks as he pulls onto the road leading away from the ranch.

"It's for kids who've had cancer. I'm a counselor there."

"Sounds sad."

"It's not."

Camp Charlie was created by Dr. Charles Schroeder, a pediatric oncologist who I've been shadowing in the hospital once a week for two years now. If I had cancer, I would want Dr. Schroeder taking care of me. Not only is he so smart that other doctors come to him for advice, he always seems to know exactly what to say to sick children and their parents to comfort them.

He considers me to be a useful member of his team of doctors and medical students, even though I have no real medical training. After my first month with him, Dr. Schroeder challenged me to develop something that would improve the quality of his little patients' lives. I came up with the idea of a "Happy Thing Book." I decorated the outside of a blank journal with colored-paper cutouts, ribbons, and glitter paint. I told Dr. Schroeder that I would give Happy Thing Books to the patients and tell them that, every day, they should write down at least one happy thing that had happened that day. So many bad things—like needle pokes—happen to cancer patients; I thought it would be nice for them to think about something happy. Dr. Schroeder liked my idea so much that he let me give my Happy Thing Book to an eight-year-old patient named Angel, a sweet little girl with long, curly, golden-brown hair who had leukemia. Every week after that, Angel would show me what she'd written in her book. Every Saturday, she wrote, "Jessica came to visit!!!"

"The last time I saw Angel she'd lost all of her hair, but she still found things to write about in her book." I remember Angel's bald head, hidden under a pink knit hat with purple flowers that her grandmother made for her "so she wouldn't catch a cold." Her skin was pale and her lips were cracked and dry, but she still gave me a smile. "Angel is coming to camp this week." Part of me is worried that she won't be the same vibrant little girl she was back then. "I hope she's … okay."

Tim pulls up in front of the camp's main building. He looks into my eyes like he wants to say something, or do something, but he doesn't say or do anything at all.

"Thanks for the ride," I say.

"Sure," Tim says.

We hop out of the truck. Tim retrieves my bike and puts it on the ground next to me. He waits while I chain my bike, walk up the steps to the building, wave goodbye, and go inside.

And then I hear him drive away.

Saturday, July 26th

"How's Angel?" Tim asks when I enter the elephant enclosure with a shovel.

I exhale, reliving the relief that flooded through me when I saw Angel hop off the bus as she arrived at Camp Charlie. "She's great! Her hair grew back, and she looks so healthy! Oh, and she still writes in her Happy Thing Book!"

"I started a Happy Thing Book myself," Tim says.

"Really?"

"Yeah."

"What'd you write in it?"

"It's personal," he says with the slightest hint of a smile.

Ryan parks an empty wheelbarrow outside the gate. "The truck's F.O.S. You guys ready to take her to the dumpster."

"What's F.O.S.?" I ask.

"Full of s—" Ryan starts.

"Elephant poop," Tim finishes, giving Ryan a scowl.

Tim, Ryan, and I pile onto the frayed leather seat of the ranch truck, and Tim drives us down the dusty, potholed road to the dumpster. He pulls up alongside the dumpster, and we hop out.

Tim helps me up onto the edge of the truck bed and Ryan shows me how to pick up a mound of poop with the pitchfork and toss it into the dumpster. Once the demonstration is over, he starts pitching at full speed. It's actually fairly-impressive to watch him fling large heaps of stinky, partially-digested hay through the air. After a few minutes, he's really sweating. "Break," he says to Tim.

Tim takes over. At first, he works much faster than Ryan, but after about five minutes, his pace slows as well. "Your turn," Tim says to me, breathlessly.

Tim hands me the pitchfork. It's the first time I've held a pitchfork, much less actually pitched anything with one. My mounds of poop are only about half as big as Ryan's and Tim's. And most of the poop slips through the wide tines before I can pitch it.

"It's tougher than it looks, isn't it?" Tim says.

"Yeah," I pant.

Ryan takes the pitchfork from me. "It takes time to get good at it," he says as he pitches. "We get a lot of practice."

After a few more rounds, during which I become slightly more proficient, Tim pitches the last of the poop into the dumpster and we hop back into the truck. We drop off Ryan at the big cat area and Tim and I go to the kitchen to wash up. After we've scrubbed our hands and arms clean, Tim tosses two empty extra-large buckets onto the floor.

"Time to feed the bears," he says.

My heart leaps with excitement. I haven't met the bears yet.

Tim rattles off a list of ingredients as I fill the buckets with omnivore chow biscuits that look like oversized dog kibble, carrots, apples, and oranges. We have to squeeze past each other in the cramped room. A refrigerator, a huge freezer, an industrial sink, and a stainless steel table take up most of the space. Once the buckets are filled to the rim with food, Tim picks up one bucket, leaving the other one for me to carry.

As we walk to the bear enclosure, my bucket seems to get heavier and heavier.

"The bears' names are Phoebe and Jay," Tim tells me. "They're siblings."

"PB and J? Like peanut butter and jelly?"

"That was what we were going to name them, but we wanted them to have names that stand alone, so we went with Phoebe and Jay."

Before we are in sight of the bears, Tim tells me to put down my bucket of food. "We're going to give them a little playtime first, while we clean the enclosure," he tells me.

I put my bucket next to Tim's and we round the corner and find the bears lounging in their swimming pool. They climb out of the pool and watch intently as Tim slides open a gate that connects their enclosure to the fenced-in arena. "Go play," he tells the bears.

As soon as he enters the arena, Jay breaks into a gallop, water dripping from his fur. Phoebe gives chase. They run the perimeter—leaping into the air every few steps—and then Phoebe tackles Jay. They roll around on the ground, coating their wet fur with dust.

Tim hands me a shovel. "Time to get to work."

We enter the empty bear enclosure, searching for poop. Tim demonstrates how to gracefully scoop up the poop by sliding the shovel underneath it in one quick motion—like the reverse of rapidly pulling a tablecloth off a table without disturbing the dishes set on top of it. I try to imitate Tim's technique, but I end up accidentally sending the poop flying away. I try again with Tim coaching me, and after a few attempts, finally get the poop on the shovel and then into the poop bucket. As we continue to work, Tim offers me tips, but my success rate is only about fifty-fifty.

Once all of the poop has been deposited in the poop bucket, we scrub everything, hose the enclosure down, and refill the water bowls and the bears' pool.

Finally, we are ready to feed the bears, but they're still chasing and tackling one another in the arena, and so Tim decides to give them a few more minutes to play.

Tim and I sit on a log outside the fence and watch Phoebe and Jay racing about.

"Did you always want to work with animals?" I ask Tim.

"Actually, I was going to be a plumber."

My curiosity rises. Tim seems to be a born animal trainer. I figured that he'd been working with them since he was a kid. "How'd you end up here?"

Tim's gaze becomes distant. "My best friend killed himself. One night, he went over to his girlfriend's house and found her in bed with another guy. He drove his car off a cliff."

I don't know what to say other than, "I'm sorry."

Tim continues, "We'd been best friends since kindergarten. We were planning to become plumbers after we graduated high school. We were going to start our own company. After he died, I had a hard time figuring out what I wanted to do with my life. A friend of mine was friends with Leslie, and Bob was looking for a new trainer. I'd never really thought about working with animals before, but it turns out, coming here was probably the best decision I've ever made."

I follow Tim's gaze to the arena. Phoebe and Jay are poking their noses through the openings in the fence, watching us.

Tim stands. "Let's give the bears their lunch."

I go off to grab the buckets of food. When I get back, Tim has the bears in two separate rooms of their enclosure, separated by a closed gate.

"You take Phoebe, and I'll take Jay," Tim says to me. "Enter, walk to the trough, pour the food, take the empty bucket, and leave. All business. Got it?"

"Got it."

I enter Phoebe's room and walk to the trough. Phoebe lumbers over to me and runs her soft, warm, wet tongue up my arm. I haven't felt any teeth, but I wonder if she might be *tasting* me.

"She licked me," I tell Tim. "Is that okay?"

Tim laughs as he pours Jay's food into the trough. "Yeah, that's okay."

Phoebe licks me again. If I were to close my eyes, I could easily imagine that she is a friendly dog, but my eyes are open and they are looking at a big, shaggy bear that probably weighs three times as much as I do. I quickly pour Phoebe's food into her trough. Phoebe stops licking me and climbs inside the trough to eat her meal. I take my empty bucket and leave, locking the gate behind me.

Safely outside the bear enclosure, I exhale, but I feel more disappointed than relieved. I wish I could have stayed with Phoebe.

As much as it scared me, I liked getting licked by a bear.

* * *

Tim and I step inside a hot, dark, stuffy shed. He pulls a leather belt off a rack and slides it around my waist. The trainers wear these belts when they work with the animals. If Tim is fitting me for a belt, that means I'm about to work with an animal! My mind swims with excitement.

Tim hangs the first belt back up and takes another belt from the rack. He slips it around my waist. "That'll do." He grabs another, larger, belt for himself, and we burst back into the fresh air.

"Which animal are we going to work with?" I ask.

"Ming," Tim answers.

Ming isn't one of the bears or the elephants; she must be a tiger, lion, or leopard.

Tim and I find Ryan in the kitchen, where he's cutting raw meat into chunks using a large, sharp-looking knife. He plops a pile of chunks into a plastic container, and the three of us head to up the big cat enclosures.

I hang the red flag, lock the gate behind us, and follow Ryan and Tim to Ming's enclosure.

Ming is a tiger!

"Is Ming a boy or a girl?" I ask. I figure it wouldn't be a good idea to crouch down and check.

"Ming is a girl," Tim answers. "And you're going to leash her." He hands me a leash and a greeting stick.

I try to keep the anxiety that is rising up my body from spreading across my face.

Tim puts his hand on my shoulder, as if he senses my apprehension. "Hold the greeting stick in your right hand and the leash in your left hand. Greet the tiger with your greeting stick and move to her left side. Move the leash fastener to your right hand. Slip the leash below her neck and fasten it above her neck. At no time should you put your hands in front of her face. Got it?"

I remember how Tim and I had rehearsed the elephants' "Arm" behavior before I did it for real. This time, the stakes seem higher.

"Can we practice first?" I ask.

"Sure," Tim says. "I'll be the tiger."

Tim immediately goes into tiger mode. He throws his body against me—rubbing his shoulder against my side—imitating a cat. He hits me a little harder than I expect him to, but I quickly recover and place my greeting stick by Tim's neck. He walks in a circle, and I move with him, positioning myself at his left side. Carefully, I slip the leash around Tim's neck and fasten it. He turns his head and pretends to nip at me, like a wild animal.

"Excellent," Ryan says to me.

"Is the tiger going to try to bite me like that?" I ask.

"She might act like she's going to, but they don't usually bite," Ryan says. "If she does open her mouth at you, keep your greeting stick between you and the tiger and say 'No' in a loud, firm voice. Don't jump away or pull back."

Ryan unleashes Tim. "When you leash the tiger, you don't want it to be loose enough that they can slide out of it. You should barely be able to slip a few fingers between the leash and the animal."

Tim returns to human mode. "Ready?"

I nod. Ryan opens the gate to Ming's enclosure, and Tim and I step inside. Ming circles us, accidentally whacking me with her long muscular tail. She walks toward the door. I stay to her left. She turns and goes the other way. I cross behind her so that I'm back on her left side. Sensing that I won't get a better opportunity, I reach forward, slide the leash under Ming's neck, and fasten the clip.

Tim slips a few fingers under the leash. "Great job!"

That was easier than leashing you, I think, but don't say it aloud.

Because no one offers to take it from me, I stay in charge of the leash as we walk Ming past the other tigers' enclosures, along the pathway that leads to the arena. Ming stops to look at one of her fellow cats. The other tiger comes to the fence and stares at her. I sense that the stare is some type of challenge.

"Forward," Tim whispers to me.

"Forward," I say.

Ming drags me forward, hard.

"Easy," I tell her.

Ming walks nicely the rest of the way to the arena. Ryan steps ahead of us and opens the gate to the arena. Once we've entered, he locks us all inside and takes the leash from me. He leads Ming to the far end.

Tim hands me one of the leather belts, and I put it around my waist. He drops the plastic container of meat into the large pouch on the back of my belt. My heart races, half excited, half terrified.

Tim grabs a hunk of meat and impales it on the end of a skinny, five-foot-long stick. He puts the stick in my free hand. Then he demonstrates how to hold my greeting stick in front of the skinny stick as if to say "Not yet."

"When you're ready to give her the treat, you move the greeting stick out of the way of the reward stick," Tim instructs me. "Once she takes the meat, you say 'All right' to let her know that you're done. Are you ready?"

"Ready!" I say, trying to sound confident.

Tim points to a platform and says, "Call Ming, and tell her to go to that platform. Use the words 'On your seat.'"

"Ready!" Tim calls out to Ryan.

Ryan unleashes Ming. My heart pounds.

"Go ahead," Tim prompts me.

"Ming, on your seat," I say in the loudest, clearest voice I can find.

Ming starts coming right to me, rather than going to the platform. She gets closer and closer. Her wide eyes look into mine. *I wish Ryan had kept her on the leash.*

"Tell her again, and gesture to the platform with your reward stick." Tim's voice instantly calms me down.

"On your seat," I say firmly.

Ming stops walking. She looks at the treat, and then

she looks back into my eyes.

"On your seat," I say gently.

Ming turns and leaps onto the platform. I finally breathe.

"Reward her," Tim coaches.

I move the end of the reward stick toward Ming's mouth. Once the meat is a few inches from her face, she snaps it up in one bite and swallows it whole.

"All right," I say.

Ryan leashes Ming and leads her away.

We do the same thing a few more times. As soon as I start to feel ever-so-slightly confident, Tim puts on his belt and slides the reward container into his pouch. He and Ryan run Ming through other behaviors, sometimes doing two different behaviors in a row before offering a reward. Tim seems so relaxed and cues the tiger so effortlessly that I realize how awkward I must have looked. I wonder whether Ming realized it was my first time.

When Tim and Ryan finish Ming's session, there's still some meat left.

"That's for Thai," Tim says.

Who's Thai?

* * *

Thai strides into the arena as if she's a queen. She is only about the size of a medium-sized dog, but Tim warns me that leopards are much trickier to work with than tigers.

Once I have meat strapped to my back, he instructs me, "Tell Thai to come. When she gets close, tell her to stay and then reward her."

I reach behind my back and grab a bloody, squishy hunk of meat. I impale it on the end of my reward stick and tell Ryan that I'm ready.

"Go ahead," Ryan says. He doesn't release the leash.

"Thai, come," I say.

Thai prances toward me. Ryan follows.

When Thai is a few steps away, I say, "Stay."

Thai continues toward me.

I back up. "Stay."

Thai continues forward.

"Hold your ground," Tim whispers. "She's testing you."

I fight the urge to back away. "Thai, stay," I say, desperately attempting to sound confident.

Thai looks at the meat. And then … she stops.

"Good," Tim approves.

I give Thai her reward. And then tell her, "All right."

Ryan leads her away.

I smile, feeling much more confident now.

"That was great," Tim says to me. "This time, have her come and then lie down."

"Thai, come," I tell the leopard.

Thai eagerly comes to me.

"Lie down," I say.

Thai doesn't.

"Lower your sticks closer to the ground. She's focused on the reward," Tim says.

I do as Tim says. "Lie down," I repeat.

Thai crouches, then, in an instant, she leaps forward and swats the meat from my stick. She snatches it up with her mouth and devours it.

"Put another reward on the stick and have her lie down," Tim says to me.

I impale another hunk of beef. "Thai, lie down," I say.

Thai doesn't move. She's staring at the meat. I'm not sure whether she even heard me. Tim places his hands over mine. A tingling passes through my hands, courses through my arms, and meets in my chest. Gently, slowly, fluidly Tim guides my sticks closer to the ground.

"Lie down," he whispers in my ear.

"Lie down," I repeat softly.

Thai places her belly on the ground, her front paws stretched out ahead of her.

"Good girl," I reward her. "All right."

I stand up. Tim stays behind me, our bodies so close that I can feel his heat.

"You've got potential," Tim says softly, and then he steps away.

As I impale another hunk of meat on my reward stick, I can't stop the thoughts from swirling in my head. What does Tim mean? Is he just being supportive or does he think that I could actually become a professional exotic animal trainer? Or maybe he is referring to something else entirely. Maybe Tim thinks that he and I have the potential to be more than the friends we're starting to become.

But I'm supposed to be a doctor. And I didn't come to the ranch to fall in love.

Saturday, August 2nd

I burst through the ranch gates and race to the elephant enclosure. I'm late!

Emily and Pongo walk over to greet me, stepping around piles of poop. The enclosure is much dirtier than I've ever seen it. *Why isn't anyone in here cleaning? Where are the trainers?*

I check the bear area. Phoebe and Jay are there in their enclosure, but there are no people in sight. I go up to the big cat area. Inside, I see Tim. Alone. The lions are in their nighttime pride group enclosures. Tim is cleaning their empty individual enclosures with a rake.

"Hey," I call to Tim.

"Hey," he calls back. "I was wondering what happened to you."

"I overslept."

Tim walks over and unlocks the gate for me. "Don't worry, there are still plenty of chores to do."

I close and lock the gate behind me. "Where is

everyone else?"

"Paul woke up with the flu. Ryan will be here soon. Why don't you start hosing down the enclosures that I already raked?"

I drag the hose to the first enclosure and wash the perch, then the floor, then the feeding trough, and then the water bowl, careful not to miss a spot.

"You're really good at that," Tim says from behind me.

I turn—startled—and accidentally spray Tim with water.

He looks down at his now wet pants and sighs.

Every cell in my body cringes with embarrassment. "I'm really sorry."

"It's no big deal," he says, but something about the way he says that fills me with dread. Tim holds out his hand. "Give me the hose."

"Why?" I ask.

"Payback."

"Okay, I deserve it." I hand him the hose.

Tim turns the hose on me, spraying me right in the center of my chest at full blast until my shirt is dripping wet.

"That isn't fair," I say, wringing out the bottom of my shirt, creating a puddle on the ground. "I only got you a little. And it was an accident. I didn't mean to—"

"Payback isn't always fair."

Tim hands me the hose. I'm surprised he trusts me with it so quickly, but I figure he knows I won't dare spray him now.

Tim looks at me. I must look like a drowned rat. His shoulders slump as if he feels bad for me. "Okay. I'm sorry about your shirt," he says.

"I'm sorry about your pants," I say.

Tim shakes his head. "No, you're right. Your spraying me was an accident. I shouldn't have—"

"That's okay. My shirt will dry."

"Until then, you can wear mine."

"I can't take your shirt."

Tim slips his t-shirt over his head. "Yes, you can."

I stare at his rippled muscles. Tim always wears loose, baggy clothes. I had no idea that his body was so … perfect.

Tim hands me his shirt and then turns away. "I'll give you privacy, so you can change."

"What if I want you to watch?" I freeze. *Did I just say that?*

Tim turns back to me. "You want me to watch?"

"I don't know," I admit.

"You shouldn't do anything you're not sure about."

"I'm *sure* I want to kiss you," I say slowly and deliberately.

Tim's eyes narrow. "Since when?"

"Since that night when you dropped me off at Camp

Charlie."

Tim smiles. "When we were sitting there in my truck, I almost kissed you."

"Why didn't you?"

"I wasn't sure you wanted me to."

"I did," I whisper. "And I still do."

Tim pulls me into his arms. His heart is beating fast, like mine. He strokes my hair away from my face. I look into his eyes and his lips press against mine, gently at first, then hungrily.

Suddenly, an alarm rings through the air.

I pull away. "What is that?"

"Wait here," Tim says, looking concerned.

"Tim." I grab his hand and look into his eyes. "I'm glad we finally kissed."

He smiles. "Me too."

Our lips meet one more wonderful time. And then Tim runs off, leaving me alone in the empty enclosure. I lean against the lion perch, trying to process what just happened.

"Jessica!" a female voice says.

I open my eyes and see my bunkmate, Lois, staring at me, her hand on my alarm clock.

"Good morning!" she says, her eyebrows raised.

Reality hits me. "Good morning," I mumble.

Lois smiles knowingly.

"What?" I ask.

"Who's Tim?"

Lois and I don't share secrets. We aren't friends. We were paired up randomly as co-counselors. No one was allowed to switch or I'm sure she would have. We go to the same high school, where Lois is one of the cool people, and I am one of the nerds. I know who she is, and she knows who I am, but neither of us really knows each other.

"I don't have time to talk," I say, climbing out of bed and grabbing my toiletries. "I can't be late for work." I told Lois that I work at an animal ranch on Saturdays, to explain why I disappear early every Saturday morning and return in the evening, smelling like animals. I'm sure she assumes I'm working with horses or cows, not tigers and bears. She already probably thinks I'm weird; I don't need to give her any more reasons to think so.

"That's okay," Lois says, "we can talk about it later."

I hope she forgets. I don't want to tell Lois about Tim.

I rush through my morning routine so fast that I get to the ranch twenty minutes early. I'm not sure what time the trainers usually arrive, so I check the elephant enclosure; no one is there except Emily and Pongo. I get an unsettling sense of déjà vu as I walk to the bear area. Only Phoebe and Jay are there. I go up to the big cat area. The red flag is still in the bucket. I peer through the fence anyway. Tim isn't there. If he was, I think I might have freaked out.

"Looking for something?" a man's voice asks from behind me.

I spin around to find Mr. North standing there. "I'm

just … looking for the trainers," I say.

"You're early. I'll send Aaron out and the two of you can get started cleaning the elephant pen."

"Thanks," I mutter, my body filling with dread. I go to the elephant barn, sit down on the bench, and wait for Aaron, hoping that he doesn't come.

Aaron and his dad live at the ranch. That way the animals are never left alone. I wonder what it's like to grow up on the grounds of an exotic animal ranch, listening to lion roars every morning and the occasional elephant trumpet. I guess a little kid would just assume that everybody lived like that, until one of his friends says one day, in a shocked voice, "You have an *elephant* at your house!" I wonder if Aaron's friends think it's cool or weird. I wonder whether he even has any friends.

Aaron finally shows up, looking at me through angry, slit-like eyes. He silently stalks into the elephant barn and emerges with an armful of hay. He dumps the hay on the ground in two piles for the elephants, grabs a wheelbarrow and a shovel, and gets to work. I pick up a shovel and join him.

"There's no need to get here early," Aaron informs me. "You're not getting graded or anything. It's just pass or *fail*."

I don't respond. I just keep shoveling.

* * *

Aaron and I have put a good dent in the cleaning by the time Tim comes through the gate.

"Good morning," Tim says to Aaron and me.

Aaron gives him a nod of acknowledgement.

My heart beats fast. *Why am I so nervous? Nothing actually happened between Tim and me outside of my dream.*

"Good morning," I say to Tim.

"Something wrong?" he asks me.

"No," I say a little too emphatically.

Aaron glances up from his work, but then quickly looks away.

Tim stares at my face like he's trying to read it. "Okay," he finally says.

Way to play it cool, Jessica.

Tim grabs a wheelbarrow and a shovel. I continue shoveling into Aaron's wheelbarrow until Paul arrives and Aaron says, "You guys good? I've got homework to do."

Homework? Over the summer?

"Yeah, we're good," Tim answers.

Aaron passes his shovel to Paul and heads back to his house.

I work side by side with Paul. He doesn't say anything. I'm grateful for the silence; it gives me a chance to consider the thoughts running through my head. What did my dream mean? Do I really want to kiss Tim?

I think maybe I do.

After we finish the morning chores, Tim and I go to the supply shed and grab belts and a reward stick. Then Tim opens a large storage bin and pulls out a bag of marshmallows.

"Marshmallows?" I ask.

"Rewards," Tim says.

"For who?"

"Guess."

The cats are rewarded with meat, and the elephants are given apples. That leaves only one choice. "The bears?"

"Correct," Tim says, emptying some of the marshmallows into a plastic container.

Tim and I find Paul cleaning the bear enclosure while Phoebe and Jay lounge lazily in the attached arena. Tim hands Paul the container of marshmallows, and Paul calls Phoebe back to the enclosure. He hand-feeds her a few marshmallows, which she takes gently, mostly using her dexterous tongue.

Tim and I put on our belts, grab greeting sticks, and enter the arena. Jay ambles over to us and starts licking Tim's bare arm vigorously. "They've been 'lickers' ever since they were babies," Tim explains to me. "They get very into it. Before you know it, they have your whole hand inside their mouth. Don't let that happen."

"Why do they lick so much?" I ask.

"We have two main theories," Tim says as he eases his hand out of Jay's eager mouth. "It could be their way of showing affection, or maybe it's just that they like the salty taste of sweat."

Paul joins us and hands me a marshmallow. "Put this between your lips, but don't bite it."

"Why?" I ask.

He smiles. "You'll see."

Anxiously, I look to Tim; he nods his approval. And so, my pulse accelerating, I put the marshmallow in my mouth.

"Jay, kiss," Paul says, pointing at me with his greeting stick.

Jay immediately stops licking Tim, and his long grizzly-bear snout moves toward me. Closer and closer. I feel hot, humid bear-breath against my face. I involuntarily blink and the marshmallow leaves my lips. When my eyes open, Jay is devouring his treat.

Tim hands me the reward stick. "Now that the two of you are acquainted, let's run through Jay's behaviors."

"Lift both of your sticks straight up in the air and say 'Big Bear!'" Tim instructs me.

I press a marshmallow onto the tip of the reward stick and do as Tim says, but Jay just stares at me.

"He's holding out for a better reward," Paul says.

"Like what?" I ask.

Tim sighs. "'Big Bear' is Jay's least favorite behavior.

Some of the trainers started adding a squirt of jelly to the marshmallow to encourage him. Eventually, Jay refused to do Big Bear unless there was jelly on the marshmallow. Jay had trained them. Now, we're working on getting Jay to do 'Big Bear' on our terms."

I stare at the massive animal in front of me. "How?"

"Try to make it sound fun," Tim suggests.

"Uh … okay." I put a huge smile on my face and say, in the most excited voice I can muster, "Hey, Jay, let's do Big Bear!"

I feel ridiculous, but Jay actually moves a little.

Encouraged, I shoot my arms in the air and repeat, "Big Bear!"

Jay shifts his weight. He heaves his upper body into the air, standing on his hind legs, towering over me.

"Good bear!" I breathe, feeling a mix of awe and primal fear.

"Now tell him 'Down' and reward him," Tim whispers to me.

"Down," I say, and Jay immediately drops down to all fours.

I offer him the marshmallow at the end of my reward stick, and he promptly devours it.

"All right," I say.

The rest of my first bear training session feels effortless. Jay swipes his claw in the air, bares his teeth, sits, lies on his side, and climbs onto a platform right on cue. When we are through, Jay licks my arm over and over again, exactly like he did to Tim.

As Jay's warm, wet tongue runs up my forearm again and again, I consider that, of Tim's licking theories, I think the affection hypothesis is most likely. And if Jay's licking is a sign of affection, the feeling is mutual.

* * *

"Let's go for a walk," Tim says to me after lunch. The way he says it, I know this isn't going to be just an ordinary walk.

"Okay." I follow Tim down the path that leads to the side exit of the ranch.

"What's going on between you and Aaron?" Tim asks. "There seems to be a lot of tension between the two of you."

My heart speeds. *Did Aaron say something to Tim about me?* "I'm pretty sure he hates me."

"Don't take it personally," Tim says. "He has a rough life. Bob is really strict with him. He pushes him extremely hard in school."

"Apparently, not hard enough if he has to go to summer school," I say.

Tim shakes his head. "Aaron isn't going to summer school because he failed anything. He's taking advanced classes at the community college. The public high school doesn't offer them, and Bob can't afford to send him to private school."

"Where's Aaron's mom? I ask.

"His mom died when he was five years old."

As we enter the field next to the ranch, Paul walks toward us. Behind him, Emily and Pongo are pulling up weeds with their trunks and popping them in their mouths. Aaron sits perched on a tall boulder at the far end, smoking a cigarette. I look at him, feeling, for the first time, a twinge of compassion. He scowls and turns away.

"Emily, come," Tim says.

Emily flaps out her ears and rushes to Tim.

"Stretch out," Tim tells her once she's close to us.

Emily places her belly flat on the ground. Tim drops to one knee by her side. He looks like he's about to propose to me. I stare at him uncertainly.

"Time for your elephant ride," he tells me.

My body tingles with excited apprehension. I remember seeing Leslie ride Pongo at the movie shoot, but I never thought I'd get the chance to try it.

Tim lets me use his thigh as a step to climb up onto Emily's back. Once I am seated he says, "Give her a hug and hang on."

Hang on? Hang on to what? Emily has no saddle or reins. I gently grab two handfuls of her wrinkly skin. I press my belly, chest, and face flat against her back. My legs grip her sides.

"On your feet," Tim tells Emily.

Emily rises. First, her front legs. My body tilts up. Then her back legs. My body tilts flat.

"You can sit up now," Tim tells me. "And scoot forward a bit."

I sit up and shakily slide into a spot just behind Emily's huge African elephant ears.

"You good?" Tim asks me.

"I'm a little scared," I admit. I'm pretty high up and don't feel very securely seated.

"Take a deep breath," Tim says. "We're going to start the *riding* part of the elephant ride, if you're up for it."

I'm not about to say no. "Okay."

"Emily, walk. Easy," Paul tells Emily.

Emily's shoulder blades move beneath my body, forcing me to constantly shift my balance to stay in place. She walks more slowly than I've ever seen her walk before. It seems like she knows it's my first time riding an elephant.

At first, Tim stays close to me, but after a few minutes—probably once he feels reassured that I'm doing okay—he drifts away. When we are halfway around the field, Emily suddenly stops and jerks her head a few times. It takes me a minute to realize that she's pulling up a weed with her trunk. I feel the weed give as she unearths it. As she starts forward again, Pongo joins us, walking by Emily's side, moving just as slowly as she is.

Once we've made a full loop around the field, Paul

guides Emily toward the side gate to the ranch. I glance back at Tim, who is walking, his arm wrapped in Pongo's trunk, behind us. Out of the corner of my eye, I see the boulder where Aaron had been sitting. No one is there now. I'd been concentrating so hard on my elephant ride that I didn't see him go.

As we reenter the ranch, I duck under tree branches that I never noticed before. Inside the elephant pen, Paul tells me to lie flat and asks Emily to stretch out. I hold on tightly, gripping Emily's back until she's lying on the ground. Then I jump down from Emily's back and watch her rise to her feet.

Paul hands me two apples. Emily and Pongo pluck them from my outstretched hands with the tips of their trunks and toss them into their mouths.

I look into one of Emily's bright eyes draped with long lashes. "Thank you, Emily," I say. "That was incredible."

* * *

That night, when I get back to Camp Charlie, still high on my day, Lois is waiting for me.

"So," she asks, "who's Tim?"

I swear Lois to secrecy. Then I tell her about the ranch, about Tim, even about my dream.

"Tim sounds hot!" she says when I'm through.

"He is," I agree.

"Why didn't you tell me that you were working with

bears and elephants and tigers and stuff?" she asks as if I've just revealed the best secret ever.

"I thought you would think it's weird," I admit.

"It *is* weird, but it's neat," Lois says. "Look, I promised I wouldn't tell anyone what you told me, and I won't, but you should tell people about the animal ranch. If they say anything stupid about it, tell them I said it was cool."

It's kind of cocky of Lois to think that her saying that something is cool will cause everyone to instantly accept it, but I have no doubt that it's true.

Lois smiles. "So, when are you going to kiss Tim for real?"

"We're just friends," I say quickly, although I'm not sure that is entirely true.

She shakes her head. "When you do kiss him, I want to hear all about it. Deal?"

"Deal," I say. Because I'm fairly certain that I'm never going to kiss Tim.

Lois invites me to join her and her friends for dinner, and as we make a meal out of what we've scavenged from the camp kitchen, I tell them about the ranch.

"I can't believe you went in a cage with a tiger," Lois's friend Kristen says. "I would be terrified."

"Can we come visit?" Lois's boyfriend, Mark, practically begs.

"I'll ask," I promise.

Later that night, just before we go to bed, Lois says, "Mark, Kristen, Maria, Erika, and I are going on a hike tomorrow. You wanna come?"

"That'd be great," I say. I never thought I'd be hanging out with the popular people.

I turn out the light, hoping that, if I dream tonight, I dream silently.

Saturday, August 9th

Today arrived without any disconcerting Friday-night dreams, and my morning at the ranch went well. I'm getting better at shoveling and hauling. Occasionally, I feel like I'm actually helping out rather than just slowing things down. Because we finished the morning chores with time to spare, Tim, Ryan, and I took a long lunch break at the picnic table under the huge tree in the shadow of the ranch.

We are starting to wrap things up when a truck I don't recognize pulls into the parking lot. A lanky man with sun-kissed skin and short, wavy, jet-black hair pops out of the truck.

Tim introduces us, "Evan, this is Jessica. And of course you know Ryan."

Evan gives Ryan a nod and then turns to me. "Nice to meet you, Jessica."

I smile. "Nice to meet you."

"Remember, a few weeks ago," Tim says to me, "you told me you were disappointed that Bob doesn't have any monkeys at the ranch."

Of course I do. It was during that long ride to the movie set.

Evan reaches into his truck and pulls out a cage with a small monkey inside. A wave of excitement spills over me. "This is Rachel," Evan says.

As Tim, Ryan, and I walk back to the picnic table with Evan and Rachel, I learn that Evan is Bob's nephew—and Aaron's cousin. He works at Bob's brother-in-law's animal ranch, where, in addition to Rachel, they have two bears, some goats, a donkey, and a bobcat. Although Evan bears a vague physical resemblance to Aaron, Evan is so bright and pleasant that it's hard to see any similarity between them.

Tim sets out some plastic chairs. Once we're all sitting down, Evan opens Rachel's cage, and Rachel cautiously pokes her head out.

"Now, I have to warn you," Evan says to me, "Rachel is very timid and she doesn't really like strangers. But I can at least show you some of her behaviors."

Once Rachel has stepped completely out of her cage, Evan nests a rainbow-colored baby rattle inside two plastic containers with pull-off lids. He hands the puzzle to Rachel. Rachel uses her tiny fingers to pry open the first container to get to the second container and then pry open the second container to get to the toy inside. Rachel takes the toy, jumps onto the ground, walks over to me, climbs onto my chair, and nestles in my lap, like a cat wanting to be pet.

"Wow!" Evan says. "Rachel *never* goes to people she

doesn't know."

"Can I touch her?" I ask, hopeful.

Evan shakes his head. "That's probably not a good idea. Rachel can get a bit vicious if she feels threatened." Rachel doesn't look vicious at all, cuddled up in my lap clutching her baby rattle, but when I look at Tim he's biting his lower lip nervously. Evan continues, "I'm going to call her back to me."

Evan calls Rachel, and she immediately goes to him. He rewards her with a raisin, and then trades another raisin for the rattle. Then Rachel jumps down off the bench, walks over to Tim, climbs onto his chair, and grabs hold of his bottle of water.

"Looks like she's thirsty," Tim says.

Evan tosses Tim a bottle of water. "Give her this one."

Tim hands Rachel the bottle. She adeptly twists off the cap and hands it to him. Then she lifts the bottle with two hands, guiding it to her mouth as Tim stabilizes it for her. Once she's had a drink, Rachel hands Tim the bottle, jumps down, and climbs back into my lap.

Evan studies Rachel and then says, "Okay, Jessica, go ahead and try petting her. Use one hand, and give her gentle strokes on her upper back."

Given what Evan told me moments ago, I'm nervous about petting Rachel, but if I'm going to do this, I need to put aside my fears; Rachel can surely sense them. I take a quiet breath, lift one hand, and lightly run it over her coarse fur. Evan, Tim, and Ryan watch closely.

For a few minutes, Rachel lies still, letting me pet her. Then, suddenly, she sits up. Her tiny hands and then her feet grip my bare arm and she climbs to the top of my head where she plops down and begins to paw through my hair.

Evan laughs. "She's grooming you."

Once Rachel is satisfied that I'm free of insects and other nasties, her hands and feet take her down my other arm, and she cuddles once again in my lap. As I gently stroke her back, Evan tells us about Rachel's sad past.

An older woman bought Rachel online when she was just a few weeks old. The woman dressed baby Rachel up in little outfits, and treated her like a pet. But once Rachel grew up and started having normal, aggressive, adult tendencies, the woman locked her in a cage and kept her there all the time. Rachel became very anxious and would pick and bite at herself until she developed sores on her arms, legs, and tail. One of Evan's friends heard about the situation and convinced Rachel's owner to let Evan take Rachel off her hands.

"It took almost a year for Rachel to trust anyone at the ranch. It usually takes months for her to warm up to new people. I've never seen Rachel befriend someone so quickly," Evan says to me. "But she really seems to like you."

Tim gives me the warmest smile I've ever seen. "Jess is easy to like."

I must have thanked Evan a hundred times for bringing Rachel by. I can't imagine my day getting any better until Evan's truck disappears over the hill, and Tim turns to me and asks, "You up for some lion training?"

"Yeah!" I say, infused with anticipation. I haven't worked with a lion yet.

In the kitchen, Tim chops a slab of beef into chunks and slides them into a plastic container. Ryan meets us with belts and a reward stick, and we hike up to the big cat area.

Ryan and Tim leash Lindi, and Ryan walks her to the arena. Lindi keeps her belly slung low to the ground, the way my cat walks when the doorbell rings and he growls and goes to hide under the couch.

"Lions live in prides," Ryan explains. "She's nervous about leaving her pride group."

Once Lindi loses sight of the other lions, she seems to figure out where she's heading, and she wastes no time getting there. She races so enthusiastically toward the arena that Tim has to grab hold of the leash to keep Ryan from getting pulled along. *Now I know why they didn't let me walk her.*

Once we're safely inside the arena, Ryan lets Lindi off-leash. She immediately greets Tim and Ryan by throwing the side of her body against them. It's similar to how Tim "greeted" me when he played tiger and I leashed him.

Lindi approaches me, and I brace myself for impact, but she only gives me a small half-rub. Then she strides around the arena, mouth open, taking in the scents. When Lindi finally lies down on the ground, Tim tells me to put on a belt. "Call her to this mark," he instructs me.

I press a squishy hunk of raw meat onto the tip of the reward stick, tap a small rock with my greeting stick, and say, "Lindi, on your mark."

Lindi comes to the rock, touching it with her paws. Before I have time to offer her the meat, she lunges at the reward stick. She doesn't actually touch the meat, but when she lands, her paws are no longer next to the rock.

"Get her back on the mark," Tim instructs me.

"On your mark," I say firmly.

Lindi grumbles and hisses, but she puts her paws back in place, touching the rock.

"Good girl," I say. As I move the reward stick toward Lindi, she hisses, leaps at the meat, and grabs it with her teeth. Instinctively, I jump back.

"All right," Ryan says. He leashes Lindi and leads her away.

"I flinched," I say to Tim, feeling disappointed in myself.

"You did the right thing," he says. "She wasn't challenging you, she was just taking her reward. Do you want to keep going?"

"Yeah," I say.

"Okay, call her to the mark. Reward her. Then put a new reward on your stick, and tell her 'Up.' When her front paws are both in the air, reward her again."

"Ready," I tell Ryan.

He releases Lindi from the leash.

I tap the small rock. "Lindi, on your mark."

Lindi goes to the rock. I reward her quickly, before she has a chance to hiss at me, and then sink my hand into the bloody reward bucket and impale another piece of meat on my stick.

"Up!" I say.

Lindi hisses and grumbles and lifts both paws into the air.

I reward her. "All right."

As Ryan leads Lindi away, I turn to Tim. "Why is she so angry?"

"She's not," Tim says. "Some of our tigers came from a traveling circus. The circus trainers taught them to act hissy and grumbly because they thought that the more scary and fearsome the animals appeared, the more exciting the act would be for the audience."

I remember the tiger trainer who I saw at the circus when I was a little girl. His tigers didn't act angry. I was captivated by them because the trainer was *communicating* with his tigers, not *dominating* them. He and his tigers were dancing, not fighting.

"That's stupid," I say to Tim.

Tim nods. "I couldn't agree more."

Suddenly, Lindi barrels toward me. She bolts right between my legs, lifting me onto her back, and then carrying me along with her. I quickly jump to one leg and bring my other leg over her, allowing her to continue on without me. She races to a clump of grass and fervently paws through it.

"I'm sorry, Jess," Ryan says as he retrieves the leash. "I think she saw a mouse or something over there."

Tim puts his arm around my back, and a warm flutter rushes through my chest. "You okay?"

I nod and take a deep breath, trying to quiet the pounding in my chest. With Tim's arm around me, I feel so happy and safe. I don't want him to let me go.

* * *

It is almost five o'clock when Tim announces that we're done for the day. And then he asks, "Can I give you a ride home?"

Why is Tim offering to give me a ride? My mind swims with possibilities. "Sure."

Tim doesn't say anything more until we arrive at the transition from the dirt road to the paved road, a mile away from the ranch. There he pulls over and hands me a thick envelope. Inside is a stack of hundred dollar bills and a few smaller bills.

I look up at him, confused. "What is this for?"

"Leslie got your check," he says.

"Oh." I should be excited. This is the money I earned by acting in a movie. But the money in my hand is just an ugly reminder of the lie I told to get it. I put the envelope down between us. "I don't want it."

"Jess, you earned that money."

"Donate it to the ranch," I say. "I want something good to come from it."

Tim presses his lips together and then inhales slowly. "You can donate one hundred dollars to the ranch, but you need to keep the rest of the money." He looks into my eyes. "Spend it on medical school or something."

"I don't know if I'm going to go medical school anymore," I say.

His forehead creases. "Since when?"

"Since … I don't know … Since the ranch."

Tim looks at me, his face unreadable. "Well, I'm sure you'll find something positive to do with the rest of the money someday."

I hand Tim a hundred dollar bill and then stuff the rest of the cash into my pocket.

Tim drives up to the next intersection and makes a right turn.

"Camp is the other way," I say.

"I know," Tim says.

"Then where are we going?"

"You'll see."

A few minutes later, Tim pulls into a run-down strip mall. He parks his truck and jumps out. "Come on." He grabs a shopping cart and heads into the supermarket. In the produce section, he grabs four bags of carrots and says, "For the bears." Then he chooses two large watermelons. "For the elephants." He puts ten bags of apples in the cart.

"For the elephants … and the bears," I say.

Tim nods and heads to the meat department. He adds three bags of chicken pieces to the cart and proclaims, "Okay, we've spent a total of ninety-nine dollars and forty cents."

How could he possibly know that? "Are you sure?"

He smiles playfully. "You doubt me?"

We go to the register.

"That'll be ninety-nine dollars and forty cents," the woman at the register says after she finishes ringing up our purchases.

My jaw drops. *Tim must be a human calculator.*

Tim hands her the hundred-dollar bill. She holds it up to the light, wipes a marker over it, and then puts it into the cash drawer and hands Tim sixty cents.

Tim passes the change to me. I drop it into my pocket, my jaw still slack.

* * *

"You calculated that all in your head?" I ask as Tim drives

us back to the ranch. "Are you some kind of genius or something?"

"I had a 4.0 GPA in high school," he says.

"Really?"

"Why do you sound so surprised?" A tinge of hurt creeps into his voice.

I know Tim is smart about a lot of things, but I never imagined that he was good at school. "It's just that, if you're that smart, you could have gone to some great college and become anything you wanted to be."

"I *am* what I want to be," Tim says. He doesn't sound angry, just sure of himself.

Regret squeezes my chest. "I'm sorry, Tim. I think that was my dad talking."

"It's okay," he says.

"You know I think this is the coolest job ever," I say. *I really do.*

Tim parks his truck in the ranch parking lot. "Let's put this food away."

I grab two grocery bags. Tim grabs the other three. We bring the food to the kitchen and put the fruits and vegetables in the refrigerator and the chicken in freezer, then we go back for the watermelons. Tim picks up one and tells me, "Grab the other one."

I wrap my arms around the remaining watermelon and follow Tim to the elephant enclosure. When Emily and Pongo see us, they race to the gate. Tim and I step close to them.

"Trunks up," Tim whispers to me.

"Trunks up," I say.

Emily and Pongo curl their trunks up to their foreheads faster than I've ever seen them do it before.

"Good job," I say. "All right."

With the ends of their trunks, the elephants create suction against the watermelons and lift the fruit into the air. Pongo puts his into his mouth and crushes it; juice and seeds drip down. Emily holds hers above her head and then drops it. It smashes open when it hits the hard dirt, and Emily picks up the pieces one by one and devours them. When they're finished eating, Tim and I wish the elephants goodnight.

"Feel better about the money?" Tim asks me.

"Yes, I do," I say.

He takes me to the ranch office and pulls a certificate from the file cabinet. I haven't been in this office since my first day at the ranch. I remember being fascinated by the painting of the woman and the tiger cub. Again, I can't keep my eyes off it.

"Who is the woman in that painting?" I ask Tim, as he fills out the certificate.

"That's Aaron's mom," he says.

"She's beautiful," I say.

"I think Bob painted it," Tim adds.

I can't believe that anyone other than a professional

artist created that painting. The woman and the tiger look so lifelike. I feel like I could reach over and touch them. More importantly, I feel like I want to.

Tim hands me the completed certificate. "Thank you for your donation," he says with mock-formality. "Would you like a plush elephant, tiger, or bear?"

I choose the elephant.

"Okay," Tim says, back in his normal voice. "Time to go home."

That reminds me: "Some of the counselors at Camp Charlie wanted to know if they can come visit the ranch."

"You can invite them to your presentation."

"My *presentation*?"

"It's going to be on your last day of class. You'll pick three types of animals, give a little educational talk about each of them, and then demonstrate their behaviors for your guests. You can invite as many people as you want, within reason."

I hate giving presentations. The thought of standing up in front of people and talking to them while they stare at me makes me want to vomit. "Do I *have to* do a presentation?"

"It's part of the class, and it'll be fun," Tim assures me.

I dread it.

Saturday, August 16th

When I arrive at the ranch, the sky is dark, even though the sun has already risen. Thunderstorms are forecast for late this afternoon, but it looks like the sky will open up at any second.

In the elephant enclosure, Paul is shoveling poop while Leslie leans against the gate, chatting on her cell phone. I grab a shovel and head inside the enclosure. For a moment, I consider how weird it is that entering an elephant enclosure with two massive elephants inside it feels perfectly-normal feel to me now.

Paul nods hello, and then, side-by-side, we shovel in silence. Once the wheelbarrow is full, Paul takes it away to dump it into the ranch truck. The next time it fills, I dump it.

We work for over an hour, shoveling and dumping. Strangely, Leslie continues chatting on her phone animatedly without giving us so much as a glance. I haven't worked with Leslie at the ranch before, and so I've never actually seen her do any chores, but she must; it seems that everyone here puts in their fair share. Besides, if Paul and I are the only ones working, our chores will take all day.

Leslie finally finishes her phone call, but instead of grabbing a shovel, she leaves. A few minutes later, she returns with a bag of apples.

"Emily, Pongo, come." She calls the elephants to the side of the enclosure away from where Paul and I are working.

"Trunks up," she tells them.

The elephants do as she says, and she rewards each of them with an apple.

"Big ears," Leslie says.

Emily and Pongo extend their ears straight out from their heads, and she rewards them.

Leslie continues her elephant training session until she runs out of apples, then she calls out to Paul, "Let's take the truck to the dumpster."

Paul shrugs and heads to the truck to empty our last wheelbarrow full of poop.

"How's it going, Jessica?" Leslie asks as I join her on the walk to the truck.

"Good," I say. "How are you?"

"Awesome!" she says, opening the passenger-side door for me.

I climb inside and scoot to the center of the seat and Leslie gets in next to me. Paul slides into the driver's seat and takes us on the bumpy ride to the dumpster.

After we park, Paul jumps out of the truck and grabs the pitchfork. Expertly, effortlessly, he pitches elephant poop into the dumpster. I had been impressed at how well Tim and Ryan handled the pitchfork, but Paul is faster than both of them put together. He doesn't even seem to get tired.

"Oh," Leslie says to me as we watch Paul pitch, "did Tim give you the money?"

"Yes," I tell her. "Thank you."

"You'll have to give me your address for when they send residuals," she says.

"Residuals?"

Leslie exhales. "You know, the money you get when the movie goes to TV and DVD."

"Right," I say. "I remember Tim telling me something like that. By the way, where are Tim and Ryan?"

"I don't know. They're off today," Leslie answers.

Of course they are. Every Saturday that I've been here, aside from the day that we went to the movie set, there have only been two trainers. Today, Paul and Leslie are it.

Leslie's phone rings, and she walks away to answer it. I turn back toward Paul and watch him pitch. He is intensely focused. I'm sure that if I speak he won't hear me.

I miss Tim and Ryan. I feel safe when I'm with them—at least as safe as I think I can feel around wild animals. I don't feel safe with Paul. He's very hard to read, and so I'm always on edge when I'm around him. And I get the sense that Leslie has disliked me from the moment she met me, although I don't know why.

I try to stay positive. I tell myself that I am going to have a good day with Paul and Leslie, but I can't shake the feeling that things are about to go horribly wrong.

* * *

"Do you know the cues for the bear behaviors?" Leslie asks me as we enter the bear arena with Jay, armed with a container of marshmallows.

"I think so."

I suppose I didn't sound confident enough, because Leslie responds by donning the single training belt that she brought with us and demonstrating each of Jay's behaviors for me.

"You got all that?" Leslie asks me when she's through.

"Yes," I say trying to sound more confident.

"Go ahead." She passes the belt to me and then hands me the reward stick. "Pretend you're giving your presentation."

I hate the reminder that, in just three weeks, I will be standing in front of the trainers—and any guests I chose to invite—and having them stare at me while I try to work with the animals on my own.

I ask Jay to sit. He lowers his bottom to the ground, and I reward him.

"Oh, no," Leslie says to me. "His rear end wasn't touching the ground. You shouldn't have rewarded him. You're teaching him to be lazy." She grabs the reward stick from my hand and a marshmallow from the container on my back and says, "Jay, sit."

Jay sits down, his bottom a few inches from the ground.

"See what you taught him," Leslie reprimands me. "Sit," she repeats firmly to Jay.

Jay plants his bottom on the ground.

"Good sit. Good boy," Leslie says, offering Jay the marshmallow. She hands the empty reward stick back to me. "Do a L-I-E D-O-W-N," she says to me.

"Lie down," I ask Jay.

He stares at me.

"You're not commanding enough. You need to find your inner male voice," Leslie tells me.

I make my voice deeper. "Lie down."

Jay cocks his head.

"Forcefully," Leslie coaches me.

I go back to my normal voice and calmly, gently, firmly, I say, "Jay, lie down."

Jay quietly lies down on the ground.

"Good bear!" I give him the marshmallow. I wish I could hug him.

"Do B-I-G B-E-A-R," Leslie suggests.

That is Jay's least favorite behavior, and so far, we

haven't had a very good session. Tim once told me that, when you're having a tough session, you should figure out a way to turn it around and make it positive for the animal. *Maybe I should ask Jay to do one of his favorite behaviors.*

I muster all of the confidence I have and ask Leslie, "Can I do something else first?"

"What do you want to do?" she sighs.

"The swipe behavior." I claw my hand and wave it in front of my chest, giving Jay the cue.

The animals are taught to respond to both verbal and nonverbal cues, and so when Jay sees the cue, he obligingly swipes his paw in the air. *Jay loves the swipe behavior.*

"Go ahead and reward him," she huffs. "But next time you have a question about a behavior, spell it out; don't do the cue."

"Okay," I say.

Jay is watching me intently now. I look playfully into his eyes and say, "Jay, let's do Big Bear." I shoot my arms straight up.

Jay shifts his weight and then raises his upper body into air.

"Good bear!" I exclaim, surprised that he did Big Bear so easily. "And down."

Jay plops back down, and I give him his reward.

"Great," Leslie says coldly. "Let's go work Ming."

Under normal circumstances, I would be excited if one of the trainers suggested that we do a tiger training session, but now, my stomach tightens. I'm starting to feel somewhat comfortable with the elephants and the bears, but the tigers still make me nervous. The big cats often test me, and they seem to get frustrated when they can't understand my awkward cues or if I don't reward them fast enough. A tiger training session with Leslie could be torture, but I obediently follow her to the kitchen.

Leslie opens the refrigerator, pulls out a slab of raw meat and slaps it onto the cutting board. She grabs a large knife, slices off a strip of meat, and quickly cuts it into cubes. "Go ahead and cut the whole thing into chunks about this size," she says as she drops the cubed meat into a plastic reward container. "I'll be back in a little bit."

Leslie places the knife on the cutting board. I pick it up and start sawing through the meat, but I can hardly get the knife to cut. I just saw Leslie use the same knife, so I know it must be sharp enough. I try pushing harder, but that doesn't help at all.

It takes me almost thirty minutes to separate a ragged strip from the slab of meat. I've almost finished cutting the strip into frayed chunks when I hear the kitchen door open.

Leslie pops her head into the kitchen. "Ready?"

"No," I say, my cheeks hot with frustration.

Leslie picks up one of my partially-shredded chunks, shaking her head. "These are too small." She reaches into the plastic bucket and pulls out one of her neat, perfectly-shaped cubes for comparison, then she takes the knife from me and slides it across the slab, demonstrating again how to make the cubes. "Got it?"

Before I can say anything, her phone rings. She dries her hands on a paper towel as she rushes out the door.

I pick up the knife and try again, but it seems to have magically transformed from sharp to dull. I saw away pathetically at the slab. My right hand is sore. My head pounds.

All of a sudden, the knife slips, slicing into my thumb. Blood spills out of me, dripping onto the meat. My eyes burn with tears.

The kitchen door opens. I look up expecting to see Leslie, but it's Aaron.

"Did you just cut yourself?" he asks.

I tuck my thumb into my fist and wipe my eyes on my sleeve. "I'm fine."

"Let me see," he says.

Aaron walks over to me and takes my hand so gently that I let him. He turns on the faucet and rinses my thumb. I grit my teeth against the stinging until he brings my hand back out of the water. He presses a clean paper towel against the cut to blot away the blood and then examines my thumb like he's a doctor, pulling the edges of the cut away from each other and studying the wound.

"It's fairly superficial," he says. "You've had all your tetanus shots, right?"

"Yeah," I say.

Aaron puts pressure on my now-vigorously-bleeding wound with the paper towel, and we stand there together, quietly. He looks like he wants to say something. Strangely, I feel like it might be something nice, comforting even. But he doesn't speak.

When Aaron finally lifts the paper towel from my thumb, the bleeding has stopped.

"You okay?" he asks me.

"Yeah." My voice cracks a little.

He looks into my eyes. "You sure?"

Up until a few minutes ago, I wouldn't have dreamed of confiding anything in Aaron. I was sure he hated me and wanted me to fail. But after standing there with him, his hand holding mine, I feel like something has changed.

"I've been trying to cut up this meat for over half an hour, and all I've got done is one strip, and my cubes are all raggedy and too small."

"Then you're doing it wrong." He sounds like the same old Aaron again.

I'm sorry I said anything. "I'm doing it just like Leslie showed me," I argue.

"Leslie's useless," Aaron responds. "Do you want *me* to help you?"

Aaron's question must be rhetorical, because he picks up the knife, holds it against the meat, and says, "Put your hand on top of mine."

I put my hand on his.

"Now, go ahead and cut," Aaron instructs. Almost as soon as I begin, he says, "Stop!"

"What?" I ask.

"You're pushing way too hard. Here, hold the knife." Aaron hands the knife back to me and then wraps his hand around mine. This time, I cut with his guidance, and the knife makes a nice clean slice through the meat.

"Okay, go ahead and do it on your own," he says, removing his hand.

I move the knife in a light gliding motion, and it easily cuts off another perfect strip of meat. My frustration instantly evaporates.

"There you go," Aaron says washing his hands.

"Thanks," I say.

"Sure." He shoves the kitchen door open with his foot and leaves.

Alone, I quickly cube up the rest of the meat. Then I place the cubed meat in the refrigerator, clean up the work area, and wash my hands.

Leslie hasn't returned yet, and so I step outside to wait for her under the darkening sky. About fifteen minutes later, she wanders by. "Did you give up?" she calls out to me.

"No," I say. "I'm done."

Leslie marches into the kitchen and eyes the sparkling stainless steel countertop. The cutting board stands, washed, in the drying rack. She pulls the bucket of meat from the fridge, and reaches inside, taking a few chunks into her hand. She assesses them for a moment and then says, "Okay, let's go."

We arrive at the big cat area to find Paul topping off the water bowls. Leslie grabs two greeting sticks and a leash and asks me, "Do you know how to leash the tigers?"

"Yes." I feel a twinge of happiness at the memory of how Ryan and Tim had taught me by having Tim pretend to be a tiger.

"Great." Leslie hands me the leash and a greeting stick. "You can show us how it's done."

Paul opens the door to Ming's enclosure, and Leslie and I step inside.

"Hey, Ming. Chuff," Leslie says to the tiger. The trainers use the word "chuff" to engage the cats; it's an imitation of one of the happy vocalizations that tigers make.

Ming rubs against Leslie, hard, and then she approaches me. I prepare myself to greet her, moving my greeting stick into position. Suddenly, Ming snaps at me, her huge teeth inches from my chest. I jump back.

"Utt. NO!" Leslie scolds Ming.

Ming looks at Leslie and then at me. I wonder if she's going to snap at me again.

"Hurry up and leash her," Leslie says to me, sounding a bit rattled.

I want to do as Leslie says, but I'm on Ming's *right* side. I need to be on Ming's left in order to leash her. Ming eyes her perch. *I can't let Ming get on the perch.* That would put her in a dominant position, towering over us.

I head toward Ming's left side, but she turns in a circle, heading to the enclosure door.

Leslie steps forward. "Never mind. Give me the leash."

I pass the leash to Leslie, and she swiftly fastens the chain around Ming's neck.

She hands me the end of the leash. "Let's go."

Paul opens the enclosure door, and Ming bolts out, taking me with her.

"Easy," I say.

Ming slows down slightly.

"What do you think went wrong in there?" Leslie asks me.

I know exactly what went wrong: I lost my confidence.

Over these past few Saturdays, I started to feel comfortable at the ranch. I allowed myself to imagine that maybe I belong here. For the first time in a long time, I felt proud of myself ... and happy. My day with Leslie has sucked the happiness right out of me. I shouldn't have let that happen, but I wasn't strong enough to stop it.

"I don't know," I lie.

"Maybe you were overconfident," Leslie suggests.

Is she serious?

Leslie steps ahead of me and unlocks the ranch's gate. "Let's do the session out back."

As the gate swings open, Ming bounds forward. My right hand burns as the rope of her leash abrades my palm and fingers. I tighten my grip and try to brace myself, but I trip on a fallen tree branch. My elbow bangs against a rock, and tingling radiates to my fingers. When I regain sensation in my now-throbbing hand, I am no longer holding the leash, and Ming is disappearing into the wild brush at the base of the mountains that surround us.

"Are you okay?" Leslie asks me.

"Yes," I say.

"Then stand up," she barks. "We're being hunted."

I hastily scramble to my feet. Leslie, Paul, and I stand back to back to back in the center of the clearing. In the tall grass and shrubs that surround us, all is silent. It's very likely that Ming's wild instincts have kicked in and that she's crouched low, watching us, ready to pounce. And one pounce from Ming could be deadly.

Leslie impales a cube of meat on the reward stick and says, "Ming, come."

I scan the sun-withered vegetation, looking for any sign of orange and black stripes.

"Ming, come on. Chuff," Leslie repeats.

Paul holds out his hand. "Let me."

As Leslie passes him the stick, the ominous sky finally opens up. But it doesn't just begin to *rain*; it begins to *pour*. Sunscreen washes down my forehead, burning my eyes.

"Come, Ming," Paul calls out, concern seeping into his

voice.

All is quiet except for the sound of raindrops furiously falling against the plants and rocks and dirt. *What if we've lost her? What if we've lost **a tiger**?*

"Ming, come!" Paul tries again.

And then, I see a hint of orange through the grass. "There she is," I whisper.

Paul hands me the reward stick.

"Come, Ming," I say into the downpour.

Nothing happens.

"Are you sure you see her?" Leslie questions me.

"I thought I did." I wipe my eyes. In the spot where I saw Ming seconds ago, now I see just dry, dead grass. In desperation, I tap a rock on the ground with my greeting stick, producing a loud crack. Tim taught me to do that to get a distracted animal's attention.

Ming's head pops up out of the grass.

It worked!

"On your mark," I say almost reflexively.

Ming slowly walks toward us. I feel Paul and Leslie move to either side of me.

A loud clap of thunder makes Ming jump.

"You're okay," I reassure her. "On your mark."

Ming moves toward me, faster.

"Easy," Paul whispers.

"Easy," I repeat.

"When she hits her mark, reward her and then tell her

to sit," Paul says under his breath.

Ming approaches the rock that I designated as her mark. Just before her paws touch it, she leaps up and snatches the meat from the reward stick with her teeth.

"You're not in control." Leslie grabs the reward stick from me and impales a cube of meat.

"On your mark," Leslie says firmly.

Ming immediately places both paws so that they touch the rock.

"Good girl." Leslie rewards her and impales another cube of meat. "Sit."

Ming sits down.

"Good girl." Leslie rewards her and puts another cube of meat on her reward stick. "Stay."

Paul steps forward. Ming turns to watch him.

"Stay." Leslie says firmly.

There is a loud rumble of thunder. Ming cringes.

"Stay," Leslie says softly.

Paul grabs hold of Ming's soggy leash.

"Good girl. Good stay." Leslie rewards Ming. "All right."

Paul walks Ming back toward the ranch. Leslie darts ahead and opens the gate. I follow behind them all, shivering, wet, and useless.

Saturday, August 23ʳᵈ

As I chain up my bicycle and slowly walk to the elephant enclosure to start my second to last day at the ranch, I mentally prepare myself for the possibility that Leslie will be one of my trainers again today.

Inside the elephant enclosure are Emily and Pongo … and Tim!

"Hi!" Tim says to me as I approach.

"Hi!" I say, and then without considering it first, I hug him. I suppose hugging Tim hello isn't all that weird; after all, we are friends. But I hug him a little too tightly and a bit too long.

A voice tears us apart. "What is *this* all about?"

I spin around to see Leslie staring at us.

Tim keeps an arm around me as he answers, "Jess was just wishing me happy birthday."

"Right," Leslie says. And then she walks away.

I smile gratefully at Tim and run off to grab a shovel.

"Happy birthday," I say to Tim when I return. I didn't

know it was his birthday today.

"Thanks," he says as he shovels.

I follow his lead and get to work. "So how have you been?"

"Great! I've been writing in my Happy Thing Book every day. It's almost full."

"Wow! You must be a very happy person."

"It's a really small notebook. It was the only one I had lying around."

I dump a large mound of poop into the wheelbarrow. "Are you ever going to tell me what you're writing in it?"

Tim smiles hesitantly without looking up. "Maybe someday."

I keep shoveling. "Well, if you *do* want to tell me, you don't have much time. Next week's my last week."

Tim glances at me. "We'll keep in touch after that."

Warmth tinged with sadness spreads through my chest. Like most summer relationships, I know that our friendship will probably fade away with the summer, but I wish it could continue.

I walk over to another collection of poop. "Next year, I'll remember your birthday," I say. "I'll even get you a present." *I hope we still know each other next year.*

"Speaking of that, you couldn't possibly have known it's my birthday today, so what was with that greeting this morning?"

I come back to the wheelbarrow to dump my load. "I

missed you last Saturday."

Tim looks into my eyes as I empty my shovel. "I missed you too."

I smile at him and then go back for more poop. "Will you be here next Saturday?"

"I wouldn't miss your presentation day. I want to meet your friends and family."

"I'm probably not going to invite anyone."

"Why not?"

"Because ... what if I look stupid? What if I stand up there and can't think of anything to say? What if Jay refuses to do Big Bear?"

Tim shakes his head. "Your friends and family aren't going to care. All they're going to hear you say is 'Blah, blah, blah, tiger' and 'Blah, blah, blah, bear,' and they're going to be so freaking impressed that you're standing there next to that animal that they won't notice if the tiger moves her paw off the mark or if it takes a little squirt of jelly on the marshmallow to get Jay to do Big Bear." Tim hands me his shovel and strolls over to Emily. "I'll show you how simple it is." He puts on an air of authority, like a professor about to address his class. "I'm sure you all know that this is an elephant, but does anyone know whether this is an *Asian* elephant or an *African* elephant?"

Tim scans an imaginary crowd until his eyes settle on me. "Jessica?"

"African," I say quietly.

"Good." Tim beams. "And how can you tell?"

"I don't know," I say quickly.

Tim exhales. "You're not even trying."

Reluctantly, I hand Tim the shovels and take over as the speaker at his imaginary presentation. "One way to tell an Asian elephant from an African elephant is to look at their ears." I turn to Emily and say, "Let's show everyone your big ears."

Emily extends her ears out from her head, like the wings of a bird about to take flight. Tim dashes off and returns with a bag of apples. He tosses me one, and I reward Emily. Pongo eagerly joins us.

"African elephants have very large ears," I continue. "They are also, generally, much larger in body size than Asian elephants, although a big Asian elephant can be bigger than a small African elephant." I gesture to Emily and then to Pongo. "As you can see, both of these elephants have tusks. Does that help you tell whether they are male or female?"

Tim shrugs.

I smile. "That's right, Tim. Because these are African elephants, you can't tell their gender based on that. Only *male* Asian elephants have tusks, but both *male and female* African elephants can have them. Pongo is a gentleman, and Emily is a lady."

Emily crosses her back legs.

I look at her curiously. "What are you doing, Emily?"

Tim tosses me an apple. "'Be a lady' is a cue. It tells her to cross her legs."

I hand Emily the apple to reward the behavior that I accidentally cued. Then I turn to Pongo. "Pongo, you're not a lady, are you?" I shake my head vigorously, cueing him to shake his head.

Pongo shakes his head, and I reward him.

"All right, Emily and Pongo, take a bow," I say.

The elephants bow their heads.

Tim tosses me two more apples. "See, that was perfect!"

"Yeah, but it was just you," I say as I reward the elephants.

"Just me?"

"You know what I mean."

"How about we spend the rest of the day practicing for your presentation, then tonight, you invite your friends and family to come to the ranch next Saturday?" Tim suggests.

"Why do you care so much?"

He looks deep into my eyes. "I just ... don't want you to regret anything."

I wonder whether he's only talking about my presentation.

I swallow. "I'll think about it."

"I hope you do," Tim says.

* * *

Tim has an errand to do at lunchtime. I take the opportunity to go get him the perfect birthday gift: a new Happy Thing Book.

I remember seeing a small arts and crafts store in the strip mall where Tim took me to the supermarket. I ride my bike there and find a blank notebook, some dark green ribbon, stick-on letters, some safari-themed wrapping paper, scissors, and glue.

The gray-haired woman working the register asks me what I'm making as she rings up my purchases. After I explain my project to her, she offers to let me work on the book at the big table where she holds Saturday morning scrapbooking classes.

I work quickly, because I don't want to be late getting back to the ranch. Despite my rushing, the book turns out even better than I'd imagined.

"That's lovely!" the gray-haired woman exclaims looking over my shoulder. "Your boyfriend is going to like it very much!"

Tim isn't my boyfriend, but I decide not to correct her. I just say, "Thanks."

On the way back to the ranch, I let myself imagine that Tim *is* my boyfriend. It gives me a warm, content feeling deep in my chest. I wonder if he ever imagines that I'm his girlfriend.

* * *

When I get back to the ranch, there is no sign of Tim or Leslie. I sit down at the picnic table under the big, old, leafy tree with Joyce and stroke her dusty, black fur.

Suddenly, Joyce jumps up. As she dashes off, I hear the front gate open. A few seconds later, Joyce comes back around the corner with Mr. North.

"Hi, Mr. North," I say, trying not to sound disappointed.

"Bob," he corrects me. "How has your time at the ranch been?" He doesn't ask in the pleasant way that people usually ask that kind of question.

"Great," I answer. "I've learned a lot."

"Good," he continues. "This afternoon, I'd like to run through your presentation to see what you've prepared."

"Okay," I say reluctantly.

"Where are the trainers?"

"Tim had an errand. And Leslie ..." *I don't know where Leslie is.*

"That's fine. We'll get started without them."

I follow Mr. North to the kitchen. He opens the refrigerator and unwraps a slab of meat. He slaps it on a cutting board and slices it up faster than all of the trainers put together. Then he slides the cubed meat into a plastic bucket.

I follow him to the shed. As he pulls open the door, it sticks a little. The bucket of meat slips from his hand. I leap forward and catch the bucket just in time to prevent an expensive mess. And then I see something that nearly makes my heart stop: Tim and Evan lie on a blanket tossed carelessly on the shed floor … kissing. They stop and sit up. Evan grabs his shirt and pulls it over his head. I forget to breathe. My body feels numb.

"Bob, I—" Tim starts.

"That's my *nephew*!" Bob growls.

"Uncle Bob—" Evan says.

"Get out! Both of you!" Mr. North bellows. He turns to Tim. "And don't you *ever* come back."

Tim doesn't look up as he brushes by me. I want to say something, but I don't know what.

Mr. North snatches a reward stick and two leather belts from inside the shed and turns to me. "Let's go."

* * *

Mr. North marches up the hill toward the big cat area. He stops at the office and hits a button on the radio. Leslie answers.

"I need you in the big cat arena," he tells her.

"I'll be right there."

A few seconds later, Leslie comes tearing up the hill. "Where's Tim?" she asks me.

Before I can say anything, Mr. North growls, "He's gone."

Leslie looks at me accusingly.

Mr. North opens the gate to the big cat area. While I

hang the red flag, he charges ahead, stopping outside Ming's enclosure.

"I assume you've been taught to leash the cats," he says to me.

"Yes," I say. After my experience with Ming last week, I wish he had chosen any other animal to work with.

He passes the leash to me, opens Ming's enclosure, and steps inside. I join him, hoping that Ming doesn't snap at me again. Ming rubs hard against Mr. North. Adrenaline flowing, I move to Ming's left side, swiftly slip the leash around her neck, and fasten it. If I wasn't feeling so bad about what happened with Tim, I would have been relieved.

"Good," Mr. North says flatly.

Leslie opens the enclosure door, and Ming pulls me toward the arena.

"*She's* walking *you*," Mr. North says. "Keep gentle tension on the leash."

I pull back on the leash gently and try to hold that tension as best I can. Ming slows down just a bit.

"Easy. Chuff," Mr. North says softly to Ming.

Ming walks nicely the rest of the way.

Once we're safely inside the arena, Mr. North unleashes Ming. She walks the perimeter, mouth open, taking in the scents of recent visitors.

Mr. North puts on one of the leather belts and hands me the other one. I fasten it around me. The belt is way too big; it slips down below my hips. Mr. North looks annoyed.

"I'll get her another one," Leslie offers.

Mr. North nods.

When Leslie leaves, the gate clangs shut behind her, distracting Ming from her exploring. Ming comes over to Mr. North. He rubs her back affectionately, and then he walks casually over to the meat bucket that Leslie left outside the gate. He reaches through an opening, takes a handful of meat, and places the chunks in my hand.

"Go ahead. Do your tiger presentation," he instructs me, passing me the reward stick. "You can skip the introductory speech. I trust you'll have something intelligent to say."

I impale one of the meat cubes on the reward stick and tap a large stone with my greeting stick. "Ming, on your mark."

Ming walks over to the stone and places her two front paws just behind it.

"Good girl." I reward her and press another piece of meat onto the stick.

"Sit," I say.

Ming immediately sits down.

"Lie down," I say, feeling more confident.

Ming lowers herself to the ground.

And then I hear a sickening thud.

Ming jumps up.

I turn to see Mr. North lying on the ground. He looks dead. Ming walks toward him. I'm sure Ming wouldn't hurt him on purpose, but she could certainly hurt him accidentally. *I need to keep Ming away from Mr. North. I need help.*

There is a panic button in each of the arenas. Ryan pointed them out to me on my first day at the ranch. I spot the button on the opposite side of the arena; there is a tiger perch near it. I place a piece of meat on my reward stick, point at the perch with the stick, and say to Ming, "On your seat."

Ming looks confused.

I walk toward the perch, pointing to it with my reward stick. "Ming, on your seat."

Ming looks at Mr. North's body.

"Come on. Chuff. On your seat," I try again.

Ming turns and comes toward me, fast.

"Easy," I say, walking backward toward the panic button.

She's still coming fast.

"Easy. Easy, girl."

I'm close enough to the perch to tap it with my stick, which I do, but Ming comes toward *me* instead.

"On your seat," I say, trying to sound in control.

Ming swiftly jumps onto the perch, towering over me.

"Good girl." I reward her and immediately regret asking her to get up *above* me.

I press the panic button. Nothing happens. I have no idea what's supposed to happen when someone pushes it. I hadn't thought to ask Ryan that. *What if it's broken? What if Leslie got distracted? What if no one is coming to help?*

Mr. North needs CPR. I know how to do CPR, but it isn't safe to kneel on the ground and do CPR in front of a tiger. *I need to get Ming out of the arena.* I have only one cube of meat left in my hand. After that is gone, I'll have nothing to help me keep Ming away from Mr. North. *I only have one chance.*

Attached to the arena, there is a tiny enclosure with a door, but I've never seen the trainers use it. The door looks like it can be closed, but I won't know for sure until I try. I'm not sure whether Ming will be willing to go into such a small enclosure, but I have to try. It feels like the best of all of the lousy options I can think of.

I remember Tim and Paul saying "in your crate" when they led the cats into their trailers to go to the movie set, so I decide that those are the best cue words to try. I put my final cube of meat on my reward stick, my pulse pounding in my throat, and say, "Ming, in your crate."

Ming looks at me, then she looks at the arena gate, instead of the little enclosure. She must not understand that the enclosure is the "crate." I walk toward the enclosure until I can put the reward stick inside it.

"In your crate," I repeat as playfully as I can.

Ming walks to the meat. She stops at the door to the enclosure, right next to me. She tries to reach the meat with her mouth, but she can't. She looks at me, jaw open, drool dripping. *She doesn't want to go inside.*

"In your crate." *Please, Ming. Please.*

Ming steps inside with one paw and then pulls the paw back out. I move the reward stick further inside. Ming places one paw inside the little enclosure again.

"Good girl."

Ming steps inside with the other paw.

"Good girl."

I hold the reward stick as far inside the enclosure as my arm will allow. Ming moves all the way inside the enclosure to reach her reward. In an instant, she's snatched the meat from my stick. I pull back the stick and my arm, grab the door, and yank it shut. As I secure it, Ming growls deeply.

"I know, girl. I'm sorry," I say as I rush to Mr. North.

A gate slams. Leslie runs up to the arena, Aaron behind her. I kneel by Mr. North's side. His chest isn't moving. He isn't breathing. *He's dead.* I put my sweaty, bloody hands, one on top of the other, in the center of Mr. North's chest and push hard and fast.

"What the ... what happened?" Leslie asks.

"Mr. North collapsed. Call 911," I say.

Leslie pulls out her cell phone and dials.

I remember sitting in the ranch office on my very first day here, my eyes scanning the crammed walls while Mr. North ignored me. Among the photos of the animals and the trainers, the awards and certificates, and the painting of

Aaron's mother holding a baby tiger, was a little red defibrillator. I'd hardly noticed it then. But now, in my mind, it's what I notice most of all.

"Aaron, get the defibrillator from the office!" I shout.

Aaron darts away.

I keep pushing on Mr. North's chest. Before today, I'd only done CPR on a manikin in CPR class. It's strange to push like that on a real person's chest. His ribcage gives under the force of my compressions. The feeling makes me want to vomit.

"I'm going to the road to meet the ambulance," Leslie says to me, and she runs off.

I look at Mr. North's face. His eyes are slightly open, but they aren't focused on anything. Just minutes ago, his eyes intimidated me, but I'm not exactly sure that he meant them to. He was never friendly to me, but I think that was just the way he was. Animals tend to be a good judge of character, and the animals here liked and respected Mr. North; I imagine that his connection with them was a lot like the bond between the tiger trainer and the tigers I saw in the circus when I was a little girl.

After what feels like forever, Aaron runs through the gate with the defibrillator and places it on the ground next to me. I open the case and press the power button. A calm female computer voice tells me what to do.

I stick two large stickers, attached to wires that snake back to the machine, to Mr. North's chest.

"Stay clear of patient. Analyzing heart rhythm," the woman's voice says.

I hold my breath. *The machine is figuring out if it should shock Mr. North.*

The machine makes a scary, alarm-like sound, and the voice says, "Shock advised. Stay clear of patient. Press the flashing button now to deliver shock."

I move away from Mr. North and push the button. His body twitches for a split second and then lies completely still.

"Shock delivered. It is now safe to touch the patient. Resume CPR," the voice says.

It didn't work. I start pushing on Mr. North's chest again. Tears form in my eyes. *Just wake up and be okay, Mr. North! Just wake up!*

I feel a hand on my shoulder.

A uniformed man kneels next to me. "We've got him." Blue-rubber-gloved hands take the place of my hands on Mr. North's chest.

"Has he had any medical problems in the past? Heart trouble?" the paramedic asks us.

"No," Aaron responds weakly. Tears roll silently down his cheeks.

There's nothing more I can do for Mr. North, and so I go to Aaron. I put my arms around him. His body feels tense and scared. My heart hurts for him.

The paramedics talk to each other using words I don't

understand. They sound impossibly calm and in control. I wonder how they can be that way when a man is dying in front of them.

"Would someone like to come with us to the hospital?" one of them finally says.

"Go," Leslie tells Aaron. "I'll call everyone. We'll take care of everything."

Aaron hands her some keys, and we follow the gurney carrying Mr. North out of the arena. As we pass the big cat enclosures, the animals watch us, their faces up against the fences. For the first time, the paramedics seem a bit unnerved.

At the bottom of the hill, the paramedics slide Mr. North's gurney inside the ambulance. Aaron climbs in after them. Then they shut the doors and drive away quietly, lights flashing.

* * *

When the ambulance disappears from view, I turn to Leslie and ask, "What can I do to help?"

Leslie's eyes are fixed on the dirt road. "Just go home."

"Okay. But first I need to—"

"JUST GO!" Leslie says.

"First I need to take care of Ming," I say firmly. And then I march back up the hill to the big cat area.

"What?" Leslie follows me.

I stop at the locked gate. I can see Ming in the tiny enclosure attached to the arena; she claws at the door, growling, agitated.

"I put Ming in there," I say to Leslie. "Before I go, I need to get her out."

"*You* put her in there?" Leslie asks.

"Yes," I say.

"How?" she asks, shaking her head in disbelief.

"I said, 'In your crate,' and I held the reward stick inside."

"Really?"

"Really."

Leslie unlocks the gate. I go quickly to the arena and, without opening it, I drag the gate of the little enclosure open. Ming leaps into the arena.

I've seen the trainers allow animals to spend the night in the arenas, for enrichment. I am satisfied that Ming is okay now.

"Are you done?" Leslie asks.

"Yes." I walk back to the front gate and leave the ranch.

Leslie locks the gate behind me.

* * *

At Camp Charlie, I toss a few things into my backpack and tell Lois that I won't be coming back tonight.

"Where are you going?" She sounds concerned.

"Home."

* * *

In the dingy bus station waiting room, I watch the minutes tick by on a yellowed wall clock until a garbled announcement says that the bus is ready for boarding.

I climb into the bus, find a seat by the window, and watch the trees and mountains turn into bridges and buildings. Every once in a while, the bus stops. Sometimes, someone gets on or off.

One woman boards the bus and looks like she's going to sit next to me, but then she crinkles her nose and walks by. I'm still wearing my dirty ranch clothes. I didn't bother to shower and change after I left the ranch. Even though I can smell nothing, I'm certain I smell bad. Normally, I would feel self-conscious, but now, I don't care at all.

I stare out the window until we arrive at my stop. Then I get off the bus, collect my bike, ride to my house, step up to the familiar front door, and ring the bell.

My mom answers the door. Immediately, her face furrows. "Jessica, are you okay?"

I try to answer, but words won't come. I might be crying, but I'm not sure. My face feels numb. Even though I probably smell like a mix of sweat, dirt, and elephant poop, my mom wraps her arms around me and takes me into the house.

The living room is dark. A blanket lies in a heap on the

couch, and the TV flickers with the evening news. My mom clicks off the TV and hands me a box of tissues. We sit there silently. I'm sure my mom is worried. She's never seen me like this.

I finally force myself to say, "I'm … okay." But saying that opens the floodgates, and I just start talking. "Mr. North, the man who owns the ranch … I think he's dead. It happened right in front of me. I was working with a tiger and I couldn't do CPR on Mr. North until I got the tiger in a cage, but I was all by myself and it took so long. Aaron … he's Mr. North's son … Aaron got the defibrillator and I tried to use it on Mr. North. I shocked him, but it didn't get his heart started again. The ambulance came and took him away. I don't know what Aaron is going to do. Aaron's the same age as me. His dad is all he's got."

But I don't stop there, I tell my mom about my whole summer, even about Tim. She just sits and listens. When I finish saying everything there is to say, I look at her, trying to read her response.

Finally, she says, "I'm sure your friend, Aaron, appreciates what you did to help his dad."

"But it didn't work," I say, my eyes filling with tears again.

"It's easier to lose someone when you know that everything that could have been done to try to save them *was* done."

I wonder if she's thinking about Dad.

She continues, "You know, your dad got you into a CPR class when you were only six years old."

"Why did he want me to take a CPR class when I was only six?"

"*He* didn't. *You* saw a story about CPR on the morning news and were absolutely fascinated. You practiced on your stuffed animals for weeks and kept asking us if you could go to 'CPR school.' Your dad called every CPR class in the area, but they all said that you were too young. He finally found one that would accept you, but it was an hour and a half drive away, and they required that you attend with a parent or guardian. He drove you there and took the class with you."

I don't remember that.

"He must have really wanted me to be a doctor."

"He just wanted you to be happy."

"Then how come he hardly ever spent time with us?" I ask gently.

"His senior partners were very demanding. They worked late into the nights and on weekends, and they expected him to do the same. Just before he died, your dad finally got permission to take his first vacation in five years. He was planning to take us all to Orlando, because you told him that was where you wanted to go more than any place in the whole world. He was going to tell you about the trip on your birthday."

My birthday was five days after he died. I remember it

being the worst birthday ever. My mom went ahead with the party we'd planned. All of my friends came over, but there were no games or anything. We just sat around in the backyard until a deliveryman brought some pizzas. I had to bring out the cake myself, with no candles because I didn't know how to light them. After everyone left, I found my mom in her bedroom, crying.

Suddenly, I know exactly how I want to spend the rest of the money I made this summer. And then I realize that I haven't seen my little sister, Taylor, yet. She's usually buzzing around, trying to be a part of whatever is going on.

"Where's Taylor?" I ask.

"At a sleepover party."

"But she's afraid to go to sleepovers."

"Not anymore. She's been doing them all summer long. Now she's talking about going to sleep-away camp next summer. I think that's because that's where you went."

It is hard to believe that someone looks up to me that much. I never really felt like I was worth looking up to. "Let's take Taylor on vacation," I say. "I have some money."

"We can't spend your money."

"I insist."

"You're not a little girl anymore, are you?" She hugs me and then looks at me curiously. "What is that smell?"

"You don't want to know," I say, wrinkling my face. And then I hear some faint scratching at the back door. "Is that Tiger?" I don't wait for the answer. I run and open the door.

Tiger bounds into the house, barking and wagging his tail. But then he stops, perks up, and sniffs me inquisitively.

"I know," I tell him, "I smell pretty strange."

After Tiger is done sniffing me all over, I take a long hot shower, wish my mom goodnight, and then I climb into my soft, cozy bed.

Sunday, August 24th

When I open my eyes, it takes me a second to realize that I'm at home in my bedroom. My stomach sinks when I realize that the horrible nightmare echoing in my head is real.

In a chair near the window, Taylor is reading a book by the light streaming past the edge of the curtain. She looks so small, curled up with my throw pillows and stuffed animals.

Sammy is sleeping by my feet. As soon as he notices that I'm awake, he starts purring loudly.

Taylor jumps up. "You're awake! You're awake!"

"Hey, Tay."

She bounces up and down, excitedly. "What do you want to do today?"

"I have to go back to camp. There's still one more week left."

Taylor stops bouncing. "That sucks."

Taylor really missed me. The truth is, as annoying as it

can be to have a little sister who hangs on your every word and wants to be part of everything you do, I kind of missed her too.

"I brought something for you." I reach inside my backpack and pull out the stuffed elephant that Tim gave me when I made my donation to the ranch. "It's from the animal ranch."

"Did you get to train the elephants?"

"Yes. And the bears, lions, tigers, and leopards."

"When I'm sixteen, I'm gonna go there too."

I wonder whether the ranch will still be there in eight years, or even next month. If Bob is dead …

Taylor looks at me. "What's wrong?"

I shake off my thoughts. "Nothing. Why don't I make us waffles for breakfast?" Mom used to make waffles every Sunday morning, but she hasn't done that in a very long time.

"Mom's already got the waffle iron ready. She's just waiting for you to wake up to start making them. I'll go tell her you're awake." Taylor bounds out of the room.

I fall back into bed. I lie there, feeling paralyzed, staring at the walls of my bedroom, covered with pictures of my favorite actors and baby animal posters. I can't help feeling like the room belongs to someone else, someone I used to know, but not to me.

* * *

After breakfast, Taylor and I take Tiger into the backyard and throw a ball for him over and over until I'm exhausted, then Taylor, my mom, and I hop into the car, and my mom drives us to Camp Charlie. We spend the drive catching up, although I skip over a few things for Taylor's benefit.

When we arrive at camp, there's still two and a half hours before the campers will start to arrive. And so we wander along the trails, looking for birds and squirrels. Taylor pokes her head into the temporarily empty cabins, and she climbs, like a little monkey, up the rope ladder to the lookout tree house.

"There's a lake!" Taylor shouts from the tree house. "And canoes! This camp is awesome! I want to come here next summer."

I haven't told Taylor that Camp Charlie is for kids with cancer. And now isn't the time. Once Taylor climbs back down, we go out on the lake in a canoe and I teach Taylor to paddle. Before long she's paddling us around the lake while my mom and I chat softly about what a great kid she is.

"Are you talking about me?" Taylor asks as she takes a break from paddling us back toward shore.

"Yes, we are," I say. "Do you want me to take over rowing for a while?"

Taylor grins and shakes her head. "No, I got this." And then she rows even harder and faster than before.

When Taylor and my mom climb into the car to go

home, Taylor says, "This was the best day ever!"

I watch them drive off, feeling homesick for the first time all summer. Once the car is gone, before I join the other counselors to prepare for the campers' arrival, I go to the camp phone. Since cell phones don't get any reception at Camp Charlie, it's the only place to make a call. I sit down in the little office and dial the ranch's number.

After a bunch of rings, Bob's voice answers. "You have reached Bob's Exotic Animal Sanctuary. We're not available at the moment. Leave your number, and we'll call you back."

I try to figure out what I'm going to say in the second before the beep, but, instead of a beep, a computerized voice says, "This mailbox is currently full." And then the line disconnects.

I sit there, holding the receiver, wondering what is happening at the ranch. I want so badly to go there, but I know there really isn't anything I can do to help. Besides, I have responsibilities at camp. In a few minutes, I'll have a whole group of new campers counting on me.

The phone starts making weird sounds. I hang up the receiver, push thoughts about the ranch to the back of my mind, and go to greet the buses.

That night, once the happy, tired kids are in their beds, I go back to the camp phone and try calling the ranch again. The phone rings, and rings, and rings ...

Tuesday, August 26th

It's been three days now, and I still haven't been able to reach anyone at the ranch or even leave a message. I'm starting to worry that everything there is falling apart.

While Lois covers for me, I go to the camp phone. I dial the number to the ranch. The phone rings, and rings, and—

"Hello?" It's a man's voice.

"It's Jessica Rainville ..." I start.

"This is Paul."

Questions flood my mind. I don't know which one to ask first. Finally, I ask, "Is everything okay?" *Of course everything isn't okay.*

"Bob's still in the hospital," Paul says.

Bob is alive! "How is he?"

"He's in intensive care, but he's stable."

I wonder how Aaron's doing.

"Are you still there?" Paul asks.

"Yes." I want to ask whether I should come to the

ranch on Saturday and whether I'll still be giving a presentation. But my presentation seems like such an unimportant thing to ask about right now. "Should I still come to the ranch this Saturday?"

"Yeah. But can you fax the guest list for your presentation by Thursday afternoon?"

Not only am I going to go back to the ranch, but I get to invite my mom and Taylor, and my friends! I want everyone to see how special the ranch is, even if that means they are going to see me make a fool out of myself.

Paul continues, "Your guests should arrive at ten, but you should be here at seven."

"Thank you. I'll see you then."

"Goodnight," Paul responds. And then he hangs up.

Saturday, August 30th

I arrive at the ranch unsure of what to expect. I find Ryan, Paul, and Leslie in the elephant pen, working quietly. I go toward the shovels.

Ryan stops me. "We're all set here. Why don't you help Tim get the big cat arena ready?"

Tim is here? "Okay."

I'm not sure whether I'm ready to see Tim. I've been worrying about him ever since I last saw him, but now that I know he's back at work and presumably okay, I start focusing on myself. Even though I don't want to admit it, I still have feelings toward Tim, feelings I'd thought he shared, but I now know he doesn't.

Through the gate, I see Tim raking up leaves and branches that litter the ground. I want to walk away, but instead I call to him, "Want some help?"

"Yeah."

Tim comes to me and silently opens the gate. I follow him back into the arena, grabbing a rake along the way.

Entering the arena feels strange. The last time I was in here, Mr. North was dying. I look at the spot where he collapsed. I can almost still see him there.

"You all right?" Tim asks.

I shake my head. *I'm not.*

Tim takes my rake and rests it against the fence next to his. We sit down on the tiger perch near the panic button.

"How's Mr. North doing?" I ask.

"Great, thanks to you. You saved his life."

I never really liked Mr. North, but he means so much to the animals, and to the ranch. And to Aaron. "I'm glad."

"Me too."

I have to ask, "Are you gay?"

Tim takes a moment and then says, "Yeah."

Although, deep down, I knew that, now I know it for sure. Tim doesn't want to be my boyfriend. He never did, and he never will. Knowing that for sure hurts more than I expected.

"How'd you get involved with Bob's nephew?" I ask.

"It just kind of happened. The first month that I was here, Evan came to the ranch to help out while Paul was out of town. I fell in love with him the first day we met. We had this deep connection."

"You're easy to connect with," I say.

"I'm sorry I never told you. I wanted to. But no one here knew …"

"I wouldn't have told anyone," I say.

"I know." He inhales. "It's better now that it's not a secret anymore. Bob isn't too thrilled about his nephew and me being a couple, but Aaron had a talk with him, and he's starting to warm up to the idea. Strangely, the person who seems to be having the hardest time with it is Leslie. She said she'd thought I was involved with *you*. I tend to be pretty clueless about stuff like this. Did *you* think …?"

"No," I say automatically, "we're just really good friends."

Tim puts his arm around me and pulls me toward him. "Yes, we are."

I rest my head on Tim's shoulder and try to change the girlfriend-boyfriend feelings that I've been having toward Tim all summer into just really-good-friend feelings, but it's not that easy. Tears well up in my eyes.

I jump up and grab my rake. And then I just stand there, holding it like it's the only thing in the world that can keep me upright right now.

Tim slides off the perch and grabs his rake too. "Are we good?"

"Yeah, we're good."

And then we get to work.

* * *

We've almost finished the morning chores when I hear the first car pull into the ranch parking lot. I am nervous and excited. *My friends and family are about to see, first-hand, what I have told them about in stories!*

Leslie is the designated greeter, so she goes out to meet my guests. She comes back up the path with Lois, Mark, and Kristen. I offer to take them to the arena so that Leslie can greet another car that is pulling up. I walk them past some of the big cat enclosures, introducing them to the animals the way Ryan introduced them to me on my first day.

"Look at those huge paws," Lois says.

"I've never been this close to a real tiger," Kristen breathes.

Mark is speechless.

Their awe reminds me of the wonder I felt on my first days at the ranch. It's hard to believe that, just two months ago, I didn't know what it felt like to pet a tiger, ride an elephant, or get licked by a bear. I'd forgotten how standing so close to the animals, even with a fence between us, had made my heart race.

My mom and Taylor are the next to come through the gate. When we walk past the big cat enclosures, the tigers pace very excitedly, similarly to the way they do at mealtime. The tigers aren't used to little kids, and so they seem to think of Taylor as potential prey.

"Do they want to eat me?" Taylor asks.

"Probably," I say.

Taylor laughs, but I feel a little nervous.

My best friend from back home, Carrie, and her mom

and dad walk up the hill next. They just came back from their summer home yesterday and, other than a quick phone call inviting her to my presentation, Carrie and I haven't talked since the last week of school.

Carrie gives me a hug. "Did you have a good summer?"

"Yeah, did you?"

"Oh, yeah!" she whispers. From the tone of her voice, I'm pretty sure she had some kind of steamy summer romance. I'm sure she'll tell me all about it. I'm not sure yet what I'll tell her about my summer.

Finally, Dr. Schroeder arrives with his wife. When I first invited him, he thought I was joking. I'd had to show him the ranch's website, which now has a photo of me and Emily on it, before he believed me.

Once my guests are seated, I welcome everyone to my presentation, then I say, "I'll be right back."

A few minutes later, I return, walking side-by-side with Jay. Everyone gasps and then applauds. *Tim was right; I have nothing to worry about.* And then the back gate to the arena opens. Aaron pushes Mr. North, in a wheelchair, into the audience area of the arena. My guests are so focused on Jay that they don't notice. I suddenly feel very nervous.

Mr. North gives me a small, reassuring smile. I try to keep the surprise from registering on my face. I've never seen him smile before.

I take a deep breath and then spout off a few facts about bears while I cue Jay's behaviors. My pulse is pounding in my ears, so it's hard for me to hear what I'm saying. Jay seems to hear me just fine, because we do: On your seat. Tongue. Smile. Come. Sit. Lie down. On your side. On your seat. Sit up. Swipe. On your mark. Big Bear. On your seat. And finally, Kiss. Each behavior is done instantly and perfectly! Jay seems to understand that he has an audience.

When we are through, I turn to everyone. "What do you think of Jay?"

They respond with loud applause.

Jay licks my hands as I field questions.

Only two more presentations to go.

* * *

My final presentation, with Lotus, ends with a standing ovation. Even Mr. North gets to his feet; when he sits back down, he says something to Aaron and then Aaron wheels him out of the arena.

While Leslie leads Lotus back to her enclosure, Tim, Paul, and Ryan break my guests into small groups to give them tours of the ranch.

I follow along with Tim, who leads my mom and sister. My mom seems a little overwhelmed by the tour. As much as she loves animals, she's hesitant about getting too close. Taylor, however, has no fears. She declares that Thai is "the most beautiful cat in the world" and begs Tim to let her pet her. Tim says that petting Thai isn't a good idea, but he distracts Taylor from her disappointment by announcing that he has a surprise for her.

At the end of the tour, Tim makes good on his promise. He takes us into the kitchen and opens the refrigerator. "You see those big watermelons in there?" Tim asks Taylor.

Taylor leans inside the refrigerator. "Yeah."

"Do you think you can lift one of them?" Tim asks.

"I'm pretty strong," Taylor says.

Tim slides out one of the watermelons and puts it in Taylor's arms. "Come on," he tells her, "there's someone waiting for that. Mrs. Rainville, you can grab the other one if you'd like."

"Go ahead, Mom," I reassure her.

My mom grabs the other melon, and then Tim and I lead Taylor and my mom to the elephant enclosure.

"Tell them 'Trunks up,'" Tim says to Taylor.

"Trunks up!" Taylor beams.

Emily and Pongo place their trunks on their foreheads, and Tim moves Taylor and my mom into position in front of them.

"Tell them 'All right,'" Tim whispers to Taylor.

"All right!" Taylor shouts.

Emily and Pongo place the tips of their trunks onto the watermelons. They lift the melons into the air and drop them into their mouths.

"Wow! Oh, wow!" Taylor gushes. "That's so awesome!"

My mom laughs happily.

As I take in the scene before me, I realize how much Tim contributed to my experience at the ranch. He gave me so many wonderful memories, but, even more importantly, he helped me grow into someone who I never dreamed I could be; someone who I actually like. *How do I say thank you for all that? Those two words just don't feel like enough.*

Tim puts his arm around me and gives me a smile that tells me that I don't need to say anything at all. *He knows.*

＊ ＊ ＊

My mom and Taylor linger after my other guests have gone home. Ryan, Paul, and Leslie delight Taylor with stories about the animals while Taylor pets Joyce, the only animal at the ranch that she's allowed to touch. I notice that Leslie is acting a lot less horrible than she did a few weeks ago, although I'm not exactly sure why.

Aaron wheels Mr. North up the path.

"Hi, Mr. … Bob," I say.

"His name's 'Mr. Bob'?" Taylor asks me.

"No, just Bob," Bob says to her. "And who are you?"

"I'm Taylor." Taylor shakes his hand.

"Taylor's my sister," I say. "And this is my mom."

Bob takes my mom's hand. "Mrs. Rainville, it's very nice to meet you." *I didn't know Bob could be so pleasant.* Then he turns to me, and his expression becomes serious. "Jessica, from what they tell me, I wouldn't be here today if it weren't for you." He looks into my eyes. "I'd like you to consider the ranch to be your second home. You are always welcome here."

I feel my eyes moisten. "Thank you."

He puts his hand on my arm. "Thank *you*."

Silence follows, my mom mercifully breaks it, "Taylor and I should get going."

"I'll show you out," Bob says.

Taylor hugs everyone goodbye, including Bob, which catches him a bit off-guard. Then she skips down the path toward the parking lot, Joyce by her side. Aaron wheels Bob next to my mom. They chat the whole way. I wonder what they are saying.

* * *

As the final hours of the afternoon tick away, I feel an emptiness growing inside my stomach. I'm going to miss coming to the ranch every Saturday. Even though Bob invited me to come back whenever I want, until I get my driver's license, I'll have to convince my mom to drive me there. And, after the school year starts, I'll have homework and projects to do; I won't have much free time.

Since we finished our ranch chores in the morning, we

spend most of the afternoon enjoying the animals. We let Phoebe and Jay run around like crazy bears in the arena, and then, once they've worked off some of their energy, we pet their thick fur and let them lick our hands.

Then we take Jaipur, the very first tiger I ever pet, for a walk on the trails behind the ranch. I handle the leash, and Jaipur walks along nice and easy, except when she sees small animals scurry into the bushes. When we get back to the ranch, Jaipur lies in the grass, and I stroke her over and over again, looking at her with renewed wonder. Seeing the ranch through the eyes of my family and friends this morning reminded me how incredible this experience is.

I finally tear myself away from Jaipur when Ryan says that the elephants need a walk. Tim, Ryan, and I take Emily and Pongo to the field where we toss apples into the grass and the elephants race after them. Tim notices that my throws have gotten better.

Once our apples are gone, Tim offers me another elephant ride. Of course, I agree. Pongo stretches out, and I scramble onto his back. He walks a little faster than Emily did during my first ride, but I have grown to trust him, and so I enjoy the wild ride. Pongo gives me a ride all the way back to the ranch. When we arrive at the elephant enclosure, Tim and Ryan help me jump down while Pongo is still standing.

Then Tim says, "I have to get going."

I look at my watch. "It's only four o'clock."

"He's going to the theater this evening," Ryan says in a mock-upper-class voice.

"Evan got me tickets for my birthday," Tim explains.

"I almost forgot," I remember out loud, "I got you something for your birthday too."

"I'll be in the kitchen," Ryan says to me.

Tim and I go to the shed. I grab my backpack and pull out the gift I made for him a week ago. I never took it out of my backpack, even though, after what happened last Saturday, I didn't think I'd ever get the chance to give it to him; I was sure I'd never see him again.

"A Happy Thing Book. Made by Jessica Rainville. I love it," he says, hugging me.

"I'm going to miss you," I say softly.

"I'm going to miss you too," he says.

We hug for a very long time, but it could never be long enough, and then I watch Tim walk down the path away from the ranch.

* * *

I wipe my eyes on my sleeve and join Ryan in the kitchen, where he is slicing open packages of carnivore diet. I grab a knife and help him. When we're through, he counts the logs of meat, double-checking to make sure we have what we need, and then we load the trays into a wheelbarrow.

As we enter the big cat area, the cats greet us with fierce growls. Even though I've seen the cats' feeding behavior a few times now, I'm still a little nervous. I doubt anyone could ever get used to this. There's something very basic and instinctual about being afraid of a growling tiger.

Ryan mans the wheelbarrow and lets me toss the meat to the animals as he calls out the amounts, "Ming, one and a half. Jaipur, one. Lotus, one …"

I am careful to stay at a safe distance from the enclosures, out of the reach of excited claws, as I toss the meat to the cats. When the trays are empty and the deep growls start to subside, I rinse off at a spigot.

"Well, that's it," Ryan says. "We're all done."

As much as I hate to leave the ranch, I am ready. I go back to the shed, collect my backpack, and Ryan and I walk to the parking lot.

"I'm sure I'll see you soon," Ryan says as he gives me a quick hug.

"Thanks for everything," I say.

Ryan climbs into his truck and drives away. I unlock my bike.

Suddenly, Aaron runs into the parking lot, breathless. "Good. You're still here."

"Why?" I am concerned.

"There's something I want to show you."

"Okay." I relock my bike lock.

Aaron leads me back into the ranch. Then we walk down a path I've never taken before, the path to his house. I feel strange about walking toward Aaron's house. I've never thought about going inside, and I don't really want to, but that is exactly where Aaron is taking me. He opens the screen door and gestures for me to enter.

I walk into a neat, clean, little living room. There's a comfy-looking couch and a well-worn recliner sitting around an old TV that has an antenna sticking out of the top. On the walls are beautiful paintings, mostly of exotic animals. I wonder if Mr. North painted them.

We walk past the kitchen, where a small table and two chairs sit in the corner of an immaculate room, and head down a hallway lined with more paintings. All four of the hallway doors are closed. Part of me doesn't want to know what's behind them. I assume one of them is Aaron's bedroom. I wonder whether it's a good idea to go into Aaron's bedroom with him, alone.

Aaron opens one of the doors. "Go ahead."

I step inside. Aaron closes the door behind us. The room is pretty bare, with a cushion big enough to sleep on lying on the floor. If this is Aaron's bedroom, it is very, very strange.

Aaron walks into the half-open closet and walks out holding a baby lion. My jaw drops.

"They like to hang out in the closet," Aaron says.

"Can I touch him?" I ask.

"It's a *her*, not a *him*, but go ahead."

I reach toward the little lion and stroke her head. Her fur is soft but not as soft as I thought it would be.

"Do you want to hold her?" Aaron asks.

"Sure," I say.

"Sit down," he says. "They don't really like being held so high up."

I sit on the floor, and Aaron puts the cub into my arms. I'm glad I'm sitting down, because she's much heavier than she looked. Although she isn't much bigger than my cat, her huge paws and her weight give a hint of what she will become.

"What's her name?" I ask.

"Lerato," he says. "It means love. Leslie named her. This one's Mombasa."

I look up to see that Aaron is holding another cub.

"How many are there?" I ask.

Another furry little lion head pokes out of the closet.

"Just three," Aaron says, reaching over to rub the head of the cub in the closet. "This is Zulu."

"Where did you get them?"

"They're Savannah's. Savannah was confiscated from some idiot who was breeding lions to sell them as pets. We didn't know she was pregnant when we got her. They actually did a pregnancy test before they placed her, but it was so early in the pregnancy that it wasn't positive yet."

Lerato wriggles out of my arms and starts stalking Zulu.

"How old are they?"

"Seven weeks."

Savannah definitely didn't look pregnant on my first day at the ranch. She must have given birth just before I arrived.

"Why aren't they with their mom?" I ask.

"From the moment they were born, Savannah was completely disinterested in them. The veterinarian said that if we didn't hand-raise them they would die," Aaron explains.

Mombasa makes a strange, cat-like cry.

"It's time for their feeding," Aaron tells me. "Do you want to—?"

I don't wait for Aaron to finish. "Yes!"

Aaron leaves me alone with the cubs. Lerato pounces on Zulu. Zulu rolls onto his back and bats at Lerato with his oversized paws. Mombasa watches, wide eyed, belly to the ground, from a few feet away.

When Aaron comes back with the bottles, the cubs bound over to him. Aaron hands me one of the bottles and holds the other two for Lerato and Zulu. I hold my bottle out in front of me. Mombasa walks over, tentatively.

"She's cool, Mombasa," Aaron says to him.

Soon, Mombasa is noisily taking his dinner. His eyes glaze over. I stare at his perfect little face and the brown patches that form a speckled patterned in his sand-colored fur. When Mombasa finishes his bottle and strides off to play with Zulu, Aaron hands me Lerato's bottle as she continues to drink.

I remember something Aaron said to me on the day we first met. Now that I've had the chance to see how he interacts with the animals, it doesn't make sense, and so I ask, "Why aren't you going to go into the family business?"

"I want to be a veterinarian … if I can make it into vet school. It's supposed to be harder to get into vet school than medical school."

"You'll be a great veterinarian. They'd be making a huge mistake if they don't accept you. I mean, you're taking all those college classes—"

"How'd you know that?"

"One of the trainers mentioned it."

"I didn't know anyone knew about that. Or cared."

"They care about you. Tim totally stuck up for you when I said …" I stop myself.

"When you said what?"

"That you were a jerk. Actually, I might have said that you were a 'total jerk,'" I admit. "I was just frustrated because you hated me so much. And you didn't even know me."

"My dad allows students here so we can make some extra money, but we get a lot of spoiled rich girls who just want to get their pictures taken with the animals so they can brag to their friends. I figured you were one of them, but you're not. You're *completely* different from them." Aaron looks into my eyes. For the first time, I see tenderness inside them. "My dad is serious about you being welcome to come back here whenever you want."

"That's good, because it would be hard to say goodbye to this place. It's amazing here."

My eyes stray to Aaron's lips. I feel an overwhelming desire, almost a need, to know what they feel like. He looks at my lips, and then back at my eyes. I think he wants to kiss me. My heart races. A wonderful warm feeling envelops my body. *I want to kiss him ... so badly ...* And so I do.

Aaron's kiss is firm, but gentle. He smells like cinnamon. I wonder if he's ever kissed anyone before. I think he probably hasn't; I get the feeling that he's acting purely on instinct. The same way I am. Aaron slides his hands around my back and then down to my waist. My hands grip his arms; I can feel the muscles that hide under his t-shirt.

"Hey!" Aaron pulls away from me. He reaches behind himself and pries the bottom of his shirt out of the mouth of one of the baby lions. "No biting," he says to him.

The cub stalks off after his siblings.

"It's dangerous in here," I say.

Aaron lightly strokes the side of my face and then leans back against the wall. "Yeah."

I sit next to him, our bodies touching just barely, and we talk: about his life and mine, about his mother and my father, about school and friends, and about our summers.

One by one, the little lions pile up in the center of the

big cushion to sleep. Aaron and I curl up next to them. I rest my head on Aaron's chest.

"That was my first kiss," I admit.

"Mine too," Aaron says.

"I thought so."

"Was it bad?"

"It was amazing actually. And you smell really nice."

"What did you expect me to smell like?"

"Cigarettes."

"I quit … For my dad."

"I'm glad."

I want to kiss Aaron again, but I'm just too tired. I snuggle close to him and let sleep take me.

Sunday, August 31st

Something pulls at my sock. I open my eyes and squint against the bright sunlight reflecting off bare white walls. It's morning. Aaron is asleep next to me.

I reach down and pull Lerato off of my sock, but she snatches it up again with her little teeth and attaches herself to my boot with her claws.

Aaron opens his eyes and focuses them. "Good morning."

"Good morning," I say, wrestling my shoelaces out of Lerato's mouth.

Aaron sits up and plucks Lerato from my boot, which now has permanent little claw marks in the sole.

I check my watch. It's after seven o'clock. *My mom will be picking me up at camp in less than an hour.*

"I have to go," I say quickly. And then I look at Aaron. "I had a great time last night."

"I did too," he says.

I kiss each little lion on the head. And then Aaron and

I carefully open the door and leave the room, making sure the cubs don't follow us.

As we walk down the hallway, I ask about the paintings hanging there, "Did your dad make these?"

"My dad doesn't paint." Aaron seems amused at the thought of it.

"What about the picture in the office, of your mom with a baby tiger?"

"I painted that … from a photo that my dad took."

I can't believe that Aaron painted such a captivating picture. "You're really talented."

"Thanks," Aaron says, looking down shyly.

Bob is sitting on the recliner in the living room, reading a newspaper. "Good morning, Aaron … Jessica."

"Good morning," we say sheepishly.

Aaron and I continue toward the front door.

"Jessica, we'll see you again soon, I hope," Bob says.

"Yes, you will," I say.

Aaron and I don't say anything as we walk to the parking lot. He silently watches as I unlock my bike. Just before I go, he gives me a hug. I press my face against his chest, breathing in those final moments. When we separate, I don't look at Aaron's face. I can't.

I climb onto my bike and slowly ride the dusty road away from the ranch, finally letting tears fall down my cheeks. I'll miss the animals, and Tim, and Ryan, and even Paul, but not Leslie, and now Aaron, and maybe Bob. It will be a while before my next elephant ride, tiger petting, bear licking, and big cat feeding. Mombasa, Zulu, and Lerato will be much bigger the next time I see them.

I stop for a moment to wipe my eyes and take a final look at the ranch; it just looks like a bunch of walls from here, but I know now what is behind them.

The next time I go behind those walls, things will be different.

But sometimes, different is good.

About the author

J.W. Lynne has been an avid reader practically since birth and now writes inventive novels with twists, turns, and surprises. In the science fiction series THE SKY (ABOVE THE SKY, RETURN TO THE SKY, PART OF THE SKY, and BEYOND THE SKY), an eighteen-year-old fights to survive in a dystopian future society founded on lies. The romantic contemporary novels LOST IN LOS ANGELES and LOST IN TOKYO follow a young woman's journey after a horrible betrayal. KID DOCS dives into the behind-the-scenes action at a hospital where children are trained to become pint-sized doctors. In WILD ANIMAL SCHOOL, a teen spends an unforgettable summer working with elephants, tigers, bears, leopards, and lions at an exotic animal ranch.

43792132R00095

Made in the USA
Middletown, DE
29 April 2019